A Slanting *of the* Sun

www.transworldbooks.co.uk
www.transworldireland.ie

Also by Donal Ryan

The Spinning Heart
The Thing About December

A Slanting *of the* Sun

stories

DONAL RYAN

Doubleday Ireland

TRANSWORLD IRELAND PUBLISHERS
28 Lower Leeson Street, Dublin 2, Ireland
www.transworldireland.ie

Transworld Ireland is part of the Penguin Random House group of companies
whose addresses can be found at global.penguinrandomhouse.com

First published in the UK and Ireland in 2015 by Doubleday Ireland
an imprint of Transworld Publishers

A CIP catalogue record for this book
is available from the British Library.

ISBNs 9781781620250 (hb)
9781781620267 (tpb)

Typeset in 11/15pt Electra Light by Kestrel Data, Exeter, Devon
Printed and bound by Clays Ltd, Bungay, Suffolk

Penguin Random House is committed to a sustainable
future for our business, our readers and our planet. This book
is made from Forest Stewardship Council® certified paper.

1 3 5 7 9 10 8 6 4 2

For my parents, Anne and Donie Ryan,
with love and gratitude

CONTENTS

The Passion

SHE CRIES SOMETIMES, without noise. I know not to talk, only to leave my hand under hers on the gearstick. Where were you all the time before the court case, she asked me once, early on. In my room, I said, I slept a lot. She said she'd heard I was seen below in the Ragg and inside in Easy Street in Nenagh as bould as you like. She wasn't accusing, just telling me what she'd heard. I said I wasn't, and that was enough. You'd hear lots of things, she said. People thinking they're helping. I look sometimes at the side of her face when she cries, the straightness of the line the tears make slowly on her cheek, the red of her lips, and I want to touch her cheek, to wipe away the mark of her sorrow. But I never do.

My mother and father don't know what to say to me. Will you go back training? My shoulder, Dad, I can hardly lift a hurl with my right hand. Oh, ya, ya. Sure of course. More physio, maybe. And I say something along the lines of It's fucked for good, Dad. And he clenches his jaw and I'd say he thinks to himself He must have got that roughness in jail and God only knows what happened to him in jail and I'd say me in jail is all he thinks about ever since the day I was charged and still he won't ask me about it, never, ever. Would you not go out for a few pucks below in the field maybe or against the wall beyond and maybe it'll come right? And I say nothing and he taps his forehead with his forefinger like he doesn't know he's doing it and asks will I eat another cut of fruitcake.

They make me fries in the morning and give me plates of tart and cream and cups of scalding tea for my elevenses, as they call it, and we have dinner for lunch and dinner again for dinner and the leanness I got in jail is nearly gone. I'm melting out to fat. I'll have to do a bit of something soon that wouldn't call too heavy on my shoulder, running or soccer or something. But Bonny's brother plays for the juniors and I'd see him at training and it wouldn't be fair on him.

My mother stands and twists tea-towels in her hands as she watches birds out the back window, and gives out about the way that oul bad bitch of a cat lies in wait for them, crouched on her haunches in behind the trees. A dead wren she left on the back porch step the other day and Mam cried at the sight of it. The little darling, she said. And she wouldn't give Puss her supper no matter how much yowling she did at the kitchen window and rubbing with her paw. She can go and shite now, the murdering little rap. Then she softened a bit when Dad said She killed that bird for you, Moll, and left it there for a present for you, because she's so stuck on you. But still Puss wasn't fed.

You'll have to call out to those people, my father had said once, long before the inquest or the court. While there was still bandages on me and a cast on my arm. Why will he, PJ? My mother exploded from silence, giving him a shock. He hadn't known she was there. To see to know can he make amends in some way, to let them know how sorry he is. Lord God almighty, she said. Sorry? Sorry? Sure for the love of Jesus Christ isn't it plain to see he's sorry? What do they want? Wasn't it an accident? Tisn't as if he meant it, is it? Is it? Is it? And he never repeated himself, and I stayed in my room for most of that year, clinging to the edge of my childhood bed. They have their pound of flesh well got now, that crowd, I heard my mother say after I got out. They can put away their wounded faces. My child was taken off of me as well and he was gave back different. Toughies, that crowd.

The first day in court I pled guilty and the judge looked at me for ages before she talked. Guilty, are you? Ya, yes miss, yes ma'am, yes your honour, then I remembered the solicitor said to call her Judge. Yes, Judge. When I looked up from the floor I could have sworn she was smiling a bit at me. There was more talk and a date was given to come back. My father put his hand on my arm walking back out. Jim Gildea had called up to our house in the squad that morning even though he's meant to be retired to say there was a wild uncle over from England, the mother's brother, he had two days given on the batter inside in Limerick already, to watch out for him at the courthouse, a foxy lad, butty, wide across the shoulders. He said he'd ring the lads in Nenagh the way they'd be warned, but to be on the lookout all the same. Thanks, Jim, Dad said. Jim shook hands with me and wished me the best of luck.

It was Jim came on us that night, and he'd cried while we waited for the ambulance, and he'd held my hand and I'd whispered Bonny, Bonny, Bonny, and I couldn't move and Jim told me She's gone, son, she's gone, just keep looking, keep looking at me.

The uncle appeared from behind a pillar at the courthouse door. He had a suit on him, and he had no drink taken, the Nenagh boys said afterwards in mitigation of themselves. He even had a manila folder in his hand, as much as to say he was a lad with legitimate business with the court. He squeezed through a gap that was barely there between a cop and a solicitor, slashing sideways through the air; I felt the hot breeze of him before I properly saw him. He was a small red man with big fists and he had three digs in before I felt the first one. Four shades fell on the uncle and I was at the bottom of them and my back was flexed at an awful angle from the top step and my bad shoulder burned and when they dragged him off he was still kicking and Dad was sitting on the ground and trying to get up and there was a thin line of blood from his nose to his mouth and there was no one helping him.

The second day in court the judge made a speech about young men being in a hurry even when they were going nowhere and she asked about my apprenticeship and Bobby Mahon put up his hand and half stood with his face all red and said nearly in a whisper that I was in my third year with him and just about to get my papers and Pawsy Rogers went up to the stand and said I was a great lad and a fine hurler and a good worker and my people were the salt of the earth and he looked sideways in guilt and sorrow at Bonny's father and brother and sister and her aunts and uncles and her grandfather and still Pawsy went on that there'd be only more damage done if this boy was given a custodial sentence and there was a half a minute or so of shuffling and shouting and someone was crying and people were escorted out and the judge got a bit wicked then I think and her hammer near splintered the wood of her bench and she thanked Pawsy but she didn't sound a bit grateful and there was no mustard cut and a fella in a blue shirt and navy tie caught my elbow gently and asked into my ear did I want to go straight or go home first and I said I'd go straight and I called my mother Mammy and my father Daddy as they held me tight as pale as ghosts and the lad in the blue shirt said Okay, come on now, and as the van doors closed in the small car park at the back of the courthouse I felt a lightening inside me, a letting go, like I was stretched out flat and floating on a gentle swell.

I wasn't a week out of prison the first evening I drove out that way in the mother's Clio. I was only thinking about calling. Trying to test out the feeling I'd have if I was to call for definite, to see how much I'd shake and how sick I'd feel in my stomach. I had a jumble of words in my head, lines of things to say that wouldn't stand in any order for me. I'd thought maybe I'd write down some things and learn them off by heart, but then I had an image of myself in my head reeling off things, like a child saying tables, with my face red, getting stuck and shaking with fear and embarrassment and they all standing up looking at me, and they more embarrassed than me even and only wanting me to go away and stop reminding them of their agonies.

It was raining and she was standing by the pier of their gate wearing a mackintosh with a see-through hood pulled up over a headscarf like an oul one, waiting for a lift to town I suppose. I was shocked to see her there and slowed and stopped without thinking and wound the window down, and when I looked out and up into the rain where she stood I hadn't a word in me that was ever known and she was just as silent and her mouth shaped itself as if to speak and her green eyes widened a little bit and as mad and unexpected a thing as it was it didn't seem one bit wrong when she walked around to the passenger side. She gave a glance back to the house the way you might expect to see something or someone that might stop her or call her back to herself. But there was no one or what empty space was there didn't have enough pull on her, and she gave her head a small shake and sat in beside me and I saw she was wearing red shoes with a bit of heel and a skirt that was shorter than her loosely buttoned raincoat and she smelt like rain and cold air and perfume and soap and some other thing that made my heart beat like a madman at the wall of a padded cell. Drive out as far as the Lookout, she said, and I parked there on the hillside above the lake and we sat and looked across at the Clare Hills and the darkness falling across them. And all she said was Were you going too fast? And I said I was. And I tried not to move or make a sound as I cried and she put her hand on top of mine for the first time and something rose up inside in me, like bubbles in a bottle that was hard shook and opened too fast.

There was a prison officer who trained the Roscrea minors and he used to work in the aluminium factory with my father years ago. He was in charge of maintenance in the prison. He'd give me jobs to do during the day, scraping paint or sweeping or picking up papers, or if he'd a complicated job going on he'd leave me in my cell and say Tip away there at your oul books like a good lad. He stayed back my first night in even though he was finished his shift and brought me over to the games room and came in with me and asked did I want to play a game of pool and he pointed at a few quare hawks and said Look after this boy for me, all right? And I could hardly breathe for fear when he went away. But those lads were sound enough and I soon learned to look mostly at the floor and to stay out of things.

I told her these stories over a good few drives, about the courthouse steps and what it was like in prison, and she listened without saying anything. She hadn't known the things that had happened, or even that her brother had been home. She'd been taking things the doctor gave her to stop her going mad and they'd made her lose herself for a good long while. I told her about the watery food, the hospital smell in the corridor, the wicked-looking fucker two cells down with the scar diagonal across his face, from his chin through his lips, along his nose as far as his forehead. Even on his eyelid it was. He screamed some nights and cried like a child and three or four screws would walk him away down to the infirmary with a blanket around his shoulders. She said How did his eye survive? I didn't know. I didn't ask him. It must have been closed tight when the knife went along it. I told her about the nights spent lying there in the half-light in a bunk bed underneath a man who wouldn't pay his television licence and farted and snorted all night and loved being in prison.

I sit there and she sits there and she puts her hand on mine and sometimes it feels cold if she's been waiting for me too long. She said once, You know the way Our Lord suffered His Passion and the flesh flayed from Him? Well, that's the kind of pain I wish I felt and not this . . . this . . . And she had no name for it nor has she still. There's no words, I suppose. There's definitely none in my head, anyway. Some evenings she says nothing at all and I sit and look out through the windscreen at the lines of rain or at the sunlight that gets stuck on the smears on the glass that I keep meaning to wipe off. But her hand is always on mine and it's always warm after a minute or two and feels like it's a part of me.

She says things sometimes out of the silence suddenly, words on their own that make no sense, and then silence again. Sometimes she picks the words up again, like she's after thinking for a while about the idea that the first words represented. The heat, she said one day. Then nothing for miles. You have double it now, maybe. And Bonny has none. I can feel it off of you. Maybe it's the way you were given hers to carry. Maybe, maybe. I can feel it off you, coming from the bones of your hand, even when your hand is cold. It goes into me.

And that's all she ever said about heat. She says things now and again out of the blue that sound like questions but I can tell those days from the tone of her and the way her head is angled away from me that she's not asking anything of me. She mightn't even know she's talking out loud. I wonder what you know about me, she said one day. I wonder what Bonny had you told. Did ye talk at all to one another, I don't know. Ye were always very quiet above in her bedroom. How long were ye doing a line?

And I nearly answered her that it had been eleven and a bit months and she'd been impatient for it to be twelve and she'd wanted a Claddagh ring for our one-year, she'd had it picked out and all below in Fitzgibbon's Jewellers, but she started again talking just as I opened my mouth, saying Oh ya, sure didn't ye start going out shortly after her debs? How's it you didn't take her to her debs, I wonder. And she's wondering still because I offered no answer and nor do I think was one expected of me.

She's all I think about, all I have in my head, all day, every day. I count down the hours and minutes and seconds until I can ask for a lend of the car and lie that I'm only going for a spin or to meet the lads or to give someone a lift to training. I have a picture of her right thigh burnt into the inside of my eyes and the black tights on it and her skirt riding up along it as she sits in without a word and I feel shame at the ache in myself, I pray to God sometimes to take away the hardness, the wrongness. Sometimes we have miles driven before she speaks, if she speaks at all, or we're parked up in Castlelough looking out at the lake and the dark hills or we're in the car park of the shopping centre in Limerick or out at the Clare Glens surrounded by trees and the singing of birds. I think about her eyes and the greenness of them and her lips, swollen like they were stung by a bee. How she looks like she's crying even when she's not. About the straightness of the line the tears make slowly on her cheek, always that. About the feel of her hand on mine, the warmth of the blood pulsing through it.

Girls and their mothers are either the best of friends or else they can't bear one another as a rule, she told me. It's always either one or the other, there's no middle ground between the women. Not like the men, the way they can rub along with each other, never falling out nor being too wrapped in one another. It's all or nothing. She was only nineteen when Bonny was born. Bonny was two years younger than me. That mad bint we had for religion inside in the Brothers. She said something one day I often think of now. Mankind will evolve to the point of something. Something. Something. Apotheosis. Until then we're driven chiefly by animal wants. Is that all I am, an animal? Imagine doing these things and feeling nothing only worry about the day that's surely coming when I'll no longer be able to do these things. Sit in a car beside her, touching lightly off her, filling up with some pain that's the sweetest thing I ever felt. A still, silent animal, waiting.

I never know until I see her standing still against the high wall at the unseen end of the old mill out past Ballinaclough Cross whether she'll be there or not. Some days she is and more she isn't. And I think I'll have someday to explain to someone somewhere how I could live with it, the awful wrongness of it all, the terrible, unforgivable joy I felt each time I saw her waiting there. And Bonny dead, lovely, lovely Bonny, her daughter, and I having killed her, and I hardly remembering her face any more. I'm going to scald for an eternity in hell and I don't care.

There's a kind of a peace now in the knowing of the routes I have lying stretched away before me, only two of them, and they as clear as if they were drawn in black marker on a white page, with my present life a dot in the fork of their meeting. One is death and one is life. I'll call up to Bobby Mahon and ask to see will he take me back on for six more months and I'll sign up for my final block release inside in Limerick and once I have my papers got I'll ask her to come away with me to Canada or New Zealand or one of them places and if she says Yes I'll never be sad a day again and if she says No I'll never be sad a day again and I'll take my chances with that Lord God above of supposed infinite mercy and my mother and father will be relieved for once and for all of the burden of the worry of me. Someday soon I'll lean across and kiss her on her lips and there'll surely then be no going back from that and all that went before will just be dust.

Tommy and Moon

I RENTED A house for a year one time on the very edge of a village, and I made friends by dint of passing up and down with a man who lived on a smallholding down the road. I was meant to be writing a book but I wasn't able, and so I walked, and waited for the words to come back to me. I'd been paid an advance, and the weight of expectation attached to it had crippled me.

Tommy was up on eighty, I'd say, though he never spoke of his age. He was sprightly and lean, and he had most of his hair, and he kept it carefully combed, and he tried never to show me his pain, but I felt it. And he told me things in fits and starts, across an ancient table, in the kitchen of the cottage his grandfather built.

He was an only child, an exotic thing in the time of his youth, a thing to be speculated about, suspicious of. His parents hadn't met before their wedding day. It had all been arranged as a favour. A man met his father the evening before he got married, as he wheeled his bicycle up the long hill on his way home from town, a borrowed suit folded on his carrier.

You're getting wed tomorrow, I hear?

I am.

Who is she?

I don't know. They calls her Lorrie.

They stayed married for fifty years and died not a week apart. But that story did the rounds for generations. They calls her *Lorrie*, men would say, stretching out his mother's name, and they'd roar with laughter. Tommy would overhear the telling of it the odd time and his insides would burn and the backs of his eyes would prickle and he'd picture his mother and father and their quiet fondness, their easy love for one another. Was it an accident, he wondered, how they loved one another? Or was it God put them together, or whatever power is there behind the blueness of the sky and the blankness of eternity? Signs on there's plenty talk of mysteries in the church.

He was sent to board with the Christian Brothers. His father could just about manage the fees. There was no talk in the gospels about Jesus Christ beating children with sticks. There's talk of a devil, though, and he crossed paths with him more than once. There was one man used to rock back on his heels to get the full of the weight of his body into the swing of his leather strap and when he was doing it there was a light blazed in his eyes that was something beyond anger. Something not fully human. They sent the worst of them away off to the missions. Men that'd break bones with hurleys and have parents up in arms. Brothers that weren't circumspect enough about the subjects of their ministrations. A solicitor's son had a rib broke one time and the nephew of a monsignor had strips of flesh lifted from the palms of his hands. Men that would behave that way to the children of quality were a danger and were sent away to hot places to see would the heat sap some of their fury. Fire, though, could hardly be expected to tame the devil.

His mother used to tell him a story he loved about an aunt of hers who refused one day to stand aside at a stile for Earl Monroe and his squire, as they processed down from their estate to the village. I'll stand aside for Our Lord, if our paths ever meet, she told them, and was fired the next day from her job in the big house. She only laughed into their faces, and went to America, and married a man who organized boxing matches, and she helped him, and took over from him when he died, and became rich, and ended up a kind of an aristocrat herself.

He'd had a friend he called Moon. They'd fallen out in their boyhood and never fully made up. Moon wouldn't step in here to this house the way you do, he told me, and sit down there and drink a sup of tea. Moon was from big land, from a swanky crowd. I often met Moon on the road at the cross before Tommy's. He'd lay a cold eye on me as he passed on his bicycle, straight-backed and stately, and the odd day Tommy would be keeping an eye out for me from his garden gate and I'd hear them exchange terse comments on the weather. And Tommy would show me caricatures he'd drawn of Moon with a steady and skilful hand and he'd say, Look how stupid Moon looks in this picture. Have you ever seen anyone the like of Moon? And I'd allow that I hadn't, and he'd shake his head in mock sadness and crumple his picture and fling it into the grate. For fear at all, he'd say, and nod towards the door and wink at me.

When the Griffins were all gone, his neighbours one time on the far side from me, their house and bit of land fell to a cousin from town who set it and sold the cottage to a quare crowd. Jehovah's Witnesses. They came to his door one time and frightened him with their litany of certitudes. The things that were going to happen him, and not one thing he could do to save himself unless he was born again. Lord God, he said to them. Bad enough to have been born the once. But he hadn't the heart to run them all the same.

There was a woman he'd have liked to marry but he knew no way to cover the ground between them and nor did she.

He read a thing in a book one time about a tribe in Africa who considered themselves the rightful owners of all the cattle in the world. He thought often about them: at the mart, in the meadow, foddering the cattle he was guardian not owner of in the unknowable minds of those lean, dark, nearly naked herders. He imagined himself going to where they lived, to their plain of sand-grass and prickly bushes, circled by jungles and low hills. What would they make of him, if he rose white-faced and wellington-booted out of the undergrowth into the light of their campfire? Would they laugh at him, or welcome him, thank him for fattening their Friesians half a world away, call him Brother? Would they kill him? There now would be a death. Speared, bleeding out beneath a white hot sun. Turned quickly to carrion, flesh torn from bone by savage jaws and scything beaks. His sun-bleached skull saved to adorn a secret temple wall. He'd melt back to molecules in the bellies of beasts and be spread with their spoor across the savannah, along their ancient trails.

He said, Wouldn't that be a glorious exequy? And I was startled to quietness by the word, by his words, by the talk out of him. He said that they'd insist on burying him here, as of course they would, and incanting around his corpse, and a few words would be said beforehand and none of them truly meant, and neighbours would fidget and think about other things. And he'd only fill the bellies of worms, he'd only enrich the earth around his grave, in the hollow sunless corner of Kilscannell Cemetery where his mother and father were lowered down and covered over by silent men.

He kept a hawk once that he had found by a river on the edge of death. The wrist of its wing was too pronounced and there were balls of light shot in the mantle of it. He straightened and set the wrist of the hawk's wing with an elastic band and a strip of cardboard and plucked the shot out with tweezers and fed it bits of raw chicken and sat still and silent for days and nights with the hawk perched on his hand. The arm of an old coat he'd fashioned and sewed and used on his hand in place of the leather glove used by professionals. He tamed it by instinct and by echoes of memories of things told to him in childhood; he knew to be still, to hood the bird between meals so it would associate the sight of him with food, to gradually show the bird the world, perched all the while on his hand. He flew the hawk free when it had the full of its health back and his heart thumped until it looped around against the sun and swooped back to him. It lived with him for seven years, in the back kitchen on a stout perch he'd made from boughs of oak where it would meet his eyes sometimes and hold them, and tell him in its dark silence all the things about the world that could be known by a bird of prey, and tell him that it loved him, pure and perfect. The hawk flew in one summer evening wet with blood, full of shotgun pellets, and died. It had come back to him to see could he save it again, and he couldn't, and his breath went from him, and his reason for a time, and the world tilted a bit and never fully righted.

He couldn't ever keep a pet again after that. A few oul tabbies mooched around the yard and the odd time he fed them scraps but they never belonged to him, he never loved them, nor they him. And the few cattle came and went and he never petted them the way some do.

Time occupied him. The notion of it being a thing. How was it? All that's real is the present moment. What's a moment? A thing infinitely divisible downwards. So the smallest part of a moment doesn't exist. So a moment doesn't exist. So time doesn't exist, only as a trick the mind plays on itself to stop all things seeming to happen at once. These are the things an evening can hang on, that can give form to an hour of standing at the haggard gate, leaning, resting a foot on the second bar up, regarding thistles and bees and distant mountains with a level eye. The idea that everything has happened and nothing has happened yet, that existence is a singularity of infinite smallness, that Mammy and Daddy are still alive and were never born, that the hawk is out hunting and might come home yet.

The seeming uselessness of existing occurred often to him. The depth of the water at the bend of the river occurred often to him, where it seemed sometimes in flood to flow back on itself, to rage against its own rushing. The coils of rope in the loft of the barn, the discs of poison laid for rats. But yet each morning hope pealed from the eastern sky and rang all day in his ears, or for as much of each day as was needed.

Something will always come along, he said, to light the way a little bit. Moon, with his big roundy head up on him. The possibility that Moon might fall off of his bicycle. Ah boys. Or a book he hadn't read. Or a story he hadn't heard before. Or the shiver of a leaf, or a certain lay of light along the land. Or yourself, he said, and smiled at me, and looked away, and said no more about it.

He dreamt often of the moment of his own death. He told me once in detail about one of those dreams, and he dipped his eyes in shyness at the end of his story and brought his cup halfway to his lips before putting it down again. His hand was shaking hard. Isn't that a good one, he said. I bet you could make a right good story out of that. I bet you I could is right, I said, and smiled at him.

A pain came on him one day that rose and fell like a tidal river. He started to pass blood in the toilet and the sight of it frightened him so he stopped looking.

I saw Moon lingering by his fresh grave crying silently when all the others had gone back the road to the village to drink pints in respect and remembrance. He stood sentinel there until the sun was nearly set and I was passing back and said, Come on, Moon, I'll drop you home.

I'd been given a key and told to take a keepsake from the

cottage by the cousin who fell in for Tommy's share of this earth, after the once-over was done. I asked Moon would he come in with me. He nodded. All he'd needed all the years was an invitation.

We opened the closet beside his bed and were caught beneath an avalanche of books.

We looked at pictures he'd drawn of birds, and a painting he'd made of a hawk on a perch, with eyes of black darkness.

We read a letter he'd written to God, thanking Him for all the saving beauty in the world.

Trouble

THE WAYS OF some things are set like the blueness of the sky. The day I learnt that started with a hunt for a coil pack for the Vectra that wasn't even needed for a finish. Daddy priced one new and it was poison dear so he told your man go shite. Then he rang his cousin in Long Pavement to know had he one, and he hadn't, and Daddy rang around a few more lads he knew that had bits of scrappers lying around for breaking and there wasn't a coil pack to be got, so for a finish he gave in and rang Curley's even though he can't bear them. He said to your man on the phone If I give you a hundred euros for it and it turns out not to be what's wrong, will you take it back off of me? And your man said on the phone he would. Come on, daughter, he said to me over his shoulder as he swung into the cab of his lorry. Come with me for the spin. And of course the Vectra still wouldn't start even with the coil pack that was got from Curley's.

The Curleys have acre upon acre of scrappers. I'd love a day let free in there. There's no way in, though, bar through the front office. They have the whole place walled off like Limerick prison for fear people would be lifting stuff. They have forklifts and all in there, for piling cars on top of one another. They have a fleet of breakdown lorries and a transporter. There's a million cars in there. Daddy says God be with the days a man could give a wander about with his wrench set and get what he wanted and pay the man and go way. Besides sitting on a plastic chair in a waiting room like a man waiting for a doctor. Reception area me hole, Daddy says. It's far from reception areas the Curleys were reared. I think he had run-ins with a Curley or two in the old days.

When we went back the second time that morning to Curley's and Daddy gave his receipt in through the hatch and laid the coil pack down on the ledge in front of the hatch, I knew straight away there'd be trouble. I just had a feeling, a burning in my belly. Daddy was like a lunatic as it was because he had his hand skinned two or three times in the swapping in and out of coil packs and starters new and old and in-between and still the Vectra only coughing at him when he tried to get it going. Your man held up the receipt in front of him and his glasses was half the way down his nose and Daddy said, You're doing great examinations of it, it's not so long since you seed it last, only two or three cups of tea ago. Do you think, says your man slowly, smartly, that we dismantle cars here for the good of our health?

Well, if he did. Daddy backed back a step so he was only a kick of my leg from where I was sitting. I heard his breaths heave down his nose. Give me back ninety so, Daddy said in a low voice, real even, and we'll call it quits. That's a tenner clear for the minute it took your monkey outside to unscrew it. That's six hundred fuckin euros an hour. Nice work if you can get it, pal. Your man still had his head leaned back and he was baldy on top and curly at the sides – was he a Curley, I wonder? A person's name often describes them bang-on – and his glasses were still half the way down his snout but he was examining Daddy now instead of the receipt and he said, How's about we give you a credit note? And Daddy did his closed-mouth no-smile nose-breath laugh that he does at the start of trouble always and said, How's about you keep your word, or ninety per cent of it? And your man said No. And Daddy said, Okay, how's about I drag you out here over that counter and wipe that fuckin floor with you, and he pointed behind him at the floor, and the woman that was waiting for a catalytic converter for a 206 turned round for a look and her eyes were a kind of wide and it was then that I saw that she kind of had the look of Mary Margaret my sister I love the bones of who's gotten married and gone to England and I haven't her seen for a long time.

Then your man said, Right, and disappeared, and Daddy stood looking in through the hatch your man had closed and bolted with his two hands hanging and they changing from fists to hands and back to fists in time with the ticking of the clock. Daddy swung round from the hatch. What says that? And he pointed at a sign beside the other hatch in the far wall. Garda . . . Traffic . . . Corpse, I read out. *Core*, the 206 woman said. Hah? I nearly said as she smiled at me, and I remembered just in time and said Pardon? She had the look of Mary Margaret, for sure and certain. What about the *p* and the *s*, I said to her. They're silent, she told me. What's the point of having them there, so, I said, and she nodded and kind of laughed. It's a French word, she said. It means . . . and she wrinkled her eyes in thinking . . . branch. Like, they're the branch of the Guards that deals with traffic. This is where towed-away cars are kept, until their owners pay their fines and collect them. Oh, I said, and stayed looking at her a bit too long but she didn't see me, she was turned back around again to her magazine. Then I noticed how worried-looking Daddy was after getting. But he listened all the same to the woman explaining to me about the French *p* and *s* and he nodded at her, to say thanks, I'd say, for being so kind as to teach me something. Daddy's mad for education for me, having had none of his own. Your man was gone a good long while. There was trouble on the way, I knew.

Daddy was in an awful predicament, I also knew. He wasn't going leaving his ninety euros to the Curleys who he couldn't bear. Your man had the coil pack took back from the ledge. Daddy was after threatening violence and there was a witness. Kind as she was, and as like Mary Margaret, she would hardly lie to the shades for us. Daddy has a record as long as his two arms from before he met Mammy and she made him promise to be good. He nearly always kept his promise and when he didn't it was only because he was left with no choice. Trouble found him sometimes, no matter that he done his level best always to keep out of the path of it.

There was no knowing where your man was gone or what he was doing or who he was gone ringing. There was no knowing was there shades in behind them doors, or if they were close by, bringing in clamped cars. Probably they'd have lads that weren't shades doing that, though. But surely that hatch would be manned by shades, for the taking of the money and all off of people that was after getting towed. I knew Daddy would be having the exact same thoughts as me.

Your man arrived back and another lad with him, older and fatter and baldier with no curls. No refunds, he says, unless the part is faulty. This man said . . . Daddy started to say, pointing at the original fella, but the new lad cut him off, and said in a voice not far off a shout, and a little space between each word, He *said* he'd *take* it *back*. Ya, Daddy said, and nodded, and his shoulders relaxed a small bit. And he has it taken back, the new lad said, and he will give you a credit note in exchange, towards your next purchase. My next purchase? Daddy was all tensed up again, there was a redness rising up along his neck. My next *purchase*? Shur ye'll hardly still be here when hell is froze over, will ye? Robbing stealing lying dirty cunts is all the Curleys ever was.

The curly lad and the fat lad only stood looking, and for a finish the fat lad said, I'll be sure to pass on your feedback to them. And they both started laughing, horrible laughs, and the redness on Daddy's neck darkened and the burning in my belly got more and worse, like a fire had turned to explosion, like a car that was after getting torched will burn and then blow. The lady with the look of Mary Margaret turned again and lifted up her magazine and showed me a picture of a huge big fat one lying on a couch with one big enormous leg stretched bare out from her along the couch and the other on the ground and underneath the picture it said BRITAIN'S FATTEST WOMAN LOOKING FOR LOVE. The lady was smiling and holding the magazine up beside her face the very same as if there was no trouble in that room, and looking straight at me in an expecting kind of way. *What* do you think of her? she asked, and laughed again. Her laugh was like a lovely engine tuned perfect and just ticking over, revved nice and gentle.

And just as I kind of knew would happen without knowing I knew, Daddy went apeshit and tried to bust in through the glass of the hatch and the two lads high-tailed it and glass smashed and the shades came in all yellow and blue and when I chanced a look out of one eye they were all lying on the floor except for one shade who was standing up looking down and Daddy was roaring from underneath the small mountain of arms and legs that he was going killing every fuckin Curley there ever was. The lady with the look of Mary Margaret put her hand over mine and drew me away towards the door and we stood outside it while they held Daddy down by an arm or a leg each which was easy enough do as he had come back to himself a bit and he was going to be careful not to make his record stretch down too much farther than his two arms.

Come on, the lady said. Come on with me. She told the spare prick of a shade who did all the looking and none of the holding down of Daddy that she was with me. Daddy was cuffed and quietened and he was saying Okay, okay, go handy, I swear

I'll go and leave this place in peace and I'll pay for the broke window and all and I'm sorry for the trouble and all and if you'll let me go now there'll be no more trouble from me, I swear on the dead Martins. Them shades to a man knew who was the dead Martins. Still and all they carried him off away to the paddy-wagon.

Sometimes I look at Daddy, at his side or his back or his face, and I love him so much that it feels like he's a prize I won for doing something brilliant, better than anyone else. There's no way in hell you're ever going to hear them words out of my mouth, though. Thinking them kinds of words is enough. God hears all and knows all, and not all things need saying. I hated seeing him being dragged and he all upset, but he isn't stupid, and I knew he'd behave himself once the explosion was over. The shades probably would even deliver him home to our house or back to Curley's yard for his lorry and Mam would meet him at the door with a slap and a kiss.

The lady's car smelt plasticky and new. Janey Mac, she said. That was scary, wasn't it? Are you okay, love? Fear of me, I told her. She asked did I want a sweet and then something remembered itself in my head, something about strangers and sweets and never never getting into a car with a person not known to you. But she was pretty and she smelt so nice and even the shade with his hands hanging had only nodded and smiled at her as she'd walked me out past the trouble with my hand in hers. She was looking at me and smiling and she admired my Converses and I admired her hair and she asked where I lived and I told her Annaholty and she looked a bit confused and said What, in a house? And I said What the fuck else would I live in? and straight away put my hand over my mouth and asked God to forgive me for cursing, but only in my mind. Do you not live in a . . . have you ever lived in a . . . A what? I was right interested now. I'd never met a mad person before, only Daddy when trouble come round, but that's a different sort of mad.

A caravan.

I thought of the fire-barrel in the back yard that Daddy would set ablaze the very odd night and him and his pals would stand around it and talk and shout and laugh and curse at the sky if a helicopter passed. A campfire is legit, I heard a man say once, so they can fuck off. Part of culture and custom. It's rubbish fires is illegal. And how the fuck would they know the difference? another man said, from away up there? And the first man was lepping at his own thickness and the other man's smartness but was trying not to show it while his comrades laughed and laughed. And Daddy done his best to keep peace around the barrel, saying Jimmy's right, campfires is grand, and they know by the size and the smoke and the ring of men around it standing that it's not rubbish is being burnt but wood. Them lads have special cameras to see what's far away, even through the dark of night. My daddy don't drink no more and so his temper doesn't leave him as quick and he'll only square up to a man he thinks can match him and only if that man has done him wrong. Like the lad in Curleys with his credit note. So he's a great one now for keeping peace between people. That's kind of his job, I think.

I thought Travellers as a rule lived in caravans, the lady said.

I heard loads of things, true and untrue, said for certain about me since that day, and never a trace of doubt in the sayers' voices, but said in a way that made you know the person saying it believed something about you even though they had no right in all the world to that belief. But that first time pierced me sharpest and so deep. I'd never heard words said like that before. Words that took my sameness away, and left me kind of sorry to be me.

The lady put the back of her hand against my cheek where a tear I hadn't felt coming suddenly was and then the palm of that hand on my head and I seen her look down at her hand for just a taste of a second and a flash of something like worry visited her face and disappeared again as quick. Then she rubbed the two sides of that hand against the edge of her seat and she didn't know I seen her do it because I know in my heart and soul she didn't even know she was doing it.

She talked more but I didn't really listen, wanting to know had I gone to see *Finding Nemo*, and I only nodded, and she drove me back the road to our house and every car that came against us I felt like the people was all looking at me and I felt open on the two sides of me, and like I shouldn't be in that car at all, so I sort of hugged myself to tighten myself into as small a size as I could. I asked her drop me at the end of our road and I jumped out of her car without barely saying bye and ran up to Mammy to tell her about Daddy and the Curleys and the shades, but never breathed a word about the lady, because there was no words to say what happened, only a feeling I couldn't even name.

Even though I've grown since then and will for a good few years to come, until I'm eighteen or nineteen, I'll never again walk as tall as I did before that day. Before that lady looked at me, and divided and shrunk me, and wiped me off of herself, without even knowing she was doing it. And she never thinking for a second she was anything but kind.

The ways of some things are set, like the courses of rivers or the greenness of grass, or the trouble that follows my daddy, or the hard light of knowing in people's eyes.

The Squad

THE SKY THE day we shot the boy was clear and blue. I remember seeing before I took aim at his heart a swallow dipping and rising low along the treeline before disappearing into the flashes. There was no stir from the grass or the leaves nor any rustle from the undergrowth. The boy's screams tormented no creatures only ourselves. The gag we had on him wasn't worth tuppence. John P was there, of course, and Pat Devine, and the two Brien Cutters and Martin Guiney. It was Pat brought the rifles and the ammunition and the one magazine of blank rounds and it was Martin stowed the fired rifles in plastic sheeting inside a weighted burlap sack and rowed out solo a good ways and dropped the whole lot into the black hole in Youghal Bay. The two Brien Cutters took care of the wooden post. I don't know exactly how, nor did I ever want to.

A strange thing happened in here the other day. Not that death is any stranger in this place. There was a couple over there in front of the big picture window, sitting facing one another, playing ball. Your man the physio had them given exercises to do, something like the ones he had myself and John P doing there a few months ago when John P had more of his reason. I was watching away and next thing didn't your man drop the ball and the two of them sat looking down at it and I was thinking Will I go over in the hell and give them a dig-out not to have them sitting there looking so sadly at one another when all of a shot your man put out his hand and she grabbed it and he sort of yanked her over onto his lap and I saw then that he was crying like a child and he put his two arms tight around her middle and they were cheek to cheek for a little while, a few moments just, and she went as limp as a rag-doll in his arms and I knew then that she had died. Just like that, imagine. It was a lovely thing, really. He cradled her head with his good hand and kissed her on her cheek before they carried her away from him and then he sat there in silence a while, just looking out at the rosebushes. I think I knew him once, out in the world. I think he was a decent man.

We're not in command of ourselves any more. John P wet himself a small while ago and the boy that's meant to be keeping an eye on us was too busy scratching himself to notice. John P said nothing, only tried and tried to get up. But there's a belt clamped firm around his middle today to anchor him, because he wandered yesterday and got into terrible mischief, and they're afraid of their lives he might do himself an injury. The poor misfortune had his beige slacks on; otherwise no one might have noticed. I watched the darkening as it bloomed outwards from his middle and sprouted tendrils down his legs. He knew it was happening and hadn't power enough to stem the flow. We locked eyes for a moment or two. I'll never in what's left of my days forget the look upon his face. Are you all right, John P, I whispered, but all he heard was silence, all he saw was my hand raised uselessly and the opening and closing of my dry old mouth.

The carer as he's called copped on for a finish what was after happening to John P. He was so vexed-looking I was certain sure he was going to start beating him. He cursed in some foreign language and balled his hands into fists and stood glowering down at my oldest friend and I'd bet what bit of life I've left he was imagining himself wringing poor John P's dear old neck.

Nappies. Nappies for you from now on, my friend. Look at

you. Look at you. And John P looked sorrowfully down at himself and back up at the boy and over at me and what was there to say but sorry.

Some days I watch John P foostering about, looking for his glasses or what have you, and as a rule I'll see the thing he's looking for, knocked from the arm of his chair by his elbow onto the ground, and I'll see him getting more and more frustrated with his fruitless search, and the glasses or the book or whatever it is will be lying by his foot, and I feel a hotness rising in my mind and it's all I can do at those times not to go over and grab him by the wrist and twist it until it's on the point of snapping but I never would, I only sit here instead and say inside in my head For God's sake, John P, for God's sake, John P, until he sees at last the missing thing and goes about retrieving it, a process every bit as tortuous as the search. I never would, I'm nearly sure. But one day he was rubbing his wrist and looking at me and there was fear and something like reproach in his watery eyes, I think, and I wonder did I do him an injury unknown to myself. Is that a thing that's capable of happening? I wouldn't have thought so, before the start of this retreat of reason.

It was the bones of a year after the terrible thing happened to his only daughter before any of us laid eyes on John P. And when we did we got an awful hop. The flesh was gone from him and all that was left was skin stretched tightly over bone. I watched as people forced themselves to talk to him in the parish hall and the hurling field and out at the golf club and around the town in all the places he had always been seen and known well and greeted with real warmth and affection, and they suppressing the urge to recoil from him, and their voices pitched at an unnatural frequency in forced good humour and a little quaver in their words giving away their discomfort, saying things like, Begodden John P you're looking well, you're looking fit and healthy, how are they all at home, how's . . . And they'd leave the enquiry hanging unfinished, expecting John P to pick up its loose end and tie it in a tight knot and close it off swiftly and fully but he only stood there and the stare of him was terrifying, truth be told, his eyes seeming to have increased in size as the rest of him had shrunk, and to have been filled with a wild kind of grief. In those first few months after his return from exile he only shuffled and shrugged and mumbled and whenever he turned his cadaverous face to me I nearly cried, so sorry was I for my dear friend, for the year he was after having, for the way I had left him above in isolation with his silent wife and his savaged daughter, afraid to return after that terrible solitary meeting shortly after it all happened, not knowing words to say to them or even what way to look at them.

When Jim Gildea told us the boy was getting out, six years before the end of the sentence passed that mad day inside in the court in Limerick, he couldn't meet John P's eyes; it was as though he had assumed upon himself a vicarious responsibility for the failings of the system that employed him. Good behaviour, Jim almost whispered. John P set his face and thanked Jim and said Oh Lord God, and made a show of shaking his head and revealed nothing of the fact that we already knew, we'd been contacted weeks before by the brother of a man in the know in an office of a section of a department up the country. We had plans made, and contingencies, and the tools procured to carry out the sentence we had passed in absentia on the boy. Nothing in Jim Gildea's demeanour suggested he suspected the convening of our kangaroo court; he put his hand on John P's shoulder and promised that if that boy returned to this area he wouldn't have a moment's peace, that he, Jim, would haunt him and hound him. And how likely is it he'll show his face around here? Very likely, we knew, and Jim knew it, too, but he was doing his damnedest to balm the bite of his news, to salve the wound he thought he had inflicted. We all knew of the boy, and of his mother and father, and of theirs before them, even. He had a gaggle of sisters and brothers, some flung to the four winds and some still local, and a clatter of cousins and clan all along the far end of the Ashdown Road. They all came out of the Villas, in the heart of our parish and separate from us.

They'd come to the court to root for him and to jostle and swear in the foyer and profess their love for him and decry the terrible injustice that was being done and *slag* was said and *lying bitch* and one of them got wicked shirty and was dragged away kicking to a paddy-wagon and a cat was set among the pigeons then and a skirmish threatened to expand fully into battle and we formed a circle of decent men around John P and his wife and daughter and the guards in turn ringed us and we moved in unison to the courthouse gates and into the waiting years.

That's all long years ago and I wonder often how much of it does John P know still. There's days he looks at me from the high-back chair beside me and it's no bother to him to sit up in it and he has long since fallen back into his flesh, though he never regained his previous healthy portliness and pallor, and he still has mostly the full use of his legs, but that's a small mercy, no mercy at all in truth, when his mind is in such retreat from him, and various of his other limbs and faculties and organs are only sporadically co-operative, and he bound in any case to his day-room chair.

John P and I were born in the same week into houses within crying distance of one another. He is my elder by three days. I'm your elder and your better, he often joked, though he deferred to me on most matters and looked up to me, I knew. Neither of us had brothers in family and so fastened ourselves harder I think into our brotherhood of friendship. When I was indentured inside in Stritch's he was bereft for a time, having no one to knock about with in the gaps between chores, and he took to bringing himself on the twelve o'clock bus from Nenagh into the city the odd day the way he could meet me at the door of the converted townhouse on O'Connell Avenue as I left to have my lunch, and more than one day I cursed beneath my breath at the sight of him, grinning up at me from the foot of the steps, and the smell of muck and milking wafting sourly up at me. But I never gave vent to my annoyance and it always turned quickly to shame in myself, and I'd treat him to his lunch and a glass of lemonade, and I'd wonder at his lingering boyishness and the differences growing between us.

These guilty feelings new and old melded themselves together in the wake of John P's troubles and isolation and the rank stew of them turned to a horrible gnawing feeling, acidy in my stomach. I was forced for a finish to grant myself respite in the giving of audience to John P's vengeful notions, to have a plan set for the inevitable day when the boy who raped his daughter almost to death would be freed from prison. If only I'd gone up weekly to see him, or fortnightly, or monthly even, for God's sake, to stand in his yard and taste the air with him, to suffer the terrible silence of the kitchen where his wife and daughter were yoked and shackled by fear and sorrow and an imposturous shame, to try to see could I stem the rising tide of his rage and encourage the ebbing of it, to instil in him the notion that on this temporal plane there would be no true justice, but that all of the inequities suffered by the just would be repaid in the infinity to come, that all deficits would be closed, and Our Lord would be the leveller, not us, not us men.

John P was careful about who he spoke to of these things, that's how I judged the seriousness of his intent. He drew around him a small group of men, all of us friends since childhood, all of us from the same townland, from nearly the same road: Pat Devine, the Brien Cutters, Martin Guiney and myself. John P's air of sorrow and fearfulness washed away from him in the moments of his planning and delegation; he assumed a flinty aspect, his cheeks were bloodless except for a coin of redness at the centre of each one, he spoke in a flat and measured tone and stated clearly what he wished done. And John P of course expected me without question to be the leader of this small squad of men, and my first worry was without foundation in reason: that six seemed to me to be an unlucky number, and that we should be either five or seven. That was the first loose thread of that unravelling.

We could all give a dozen reasons at least for doing it and none for not doing it. We met without John P, the five of us, and talked it in and out and around and kept coming back to the same thing: we'd all said we'd do it in those burning days after the crime and now John P was holding us to our words. If he ever shows his face. By Jesus. By Christ. We'll shoot the cunt. We'll bury him. We'll finish the fucker. Threats made to empty air now had become covenants. It wasn't just revenge. We had to think of all the other daughters of our parish. The mechanics of how it would be done came easily to us and were agreed upon without rancour or dissent. Three rounds each, one random magazine would be loaded only with blanks the way each man could console himself afterwards that it was he had the useless gun.

We captured that boy as he walked alone, drawing beside him in a van with a wide sliding door, grabbing him from behind and around his throat and half throttling him and punching him in the stomach and face to subdue him and we pressing down with the weight of our bodies on his legs and arms so that we could bind him hand and foot and pointing our weapons into his smeared streaked face and dragging him across gorse and bog and scrub and stone to the beam we had planted deep in the earth of that lonesome hillside and we shackled him to it and rounded him with rope and he screaming all the while through his gag, and pissing himself, and shitting himself, and his tears sopping through his blindfold, and all our violence not the product of our bravery but of our panic and our fear and our mad desire to be finished and done with what we knew by then was our folly. We stood back thirty paces. That was what we had agreed. It seemed too far, it seemed too near. It was for a finish twenty-seven, I'd say.

The boy screamed before we fired, long before, all the ways up in the van, and stayed screaming after we fired because we missed his head and heart with our first volley. The rounds pierced his shoulder and left arm and one went right the ways through the very edge of his neck. Terrible shooting, shameful. The second volley tore his blindfold from his eyes and the top of the post we had him tied to exploded into splinters and one of his eyes was replaced with a dark and gory hole. And still he screamed and his entrails were exposed. And John P fell forward from the line in a strange crouching tumble and Martin Guiney roared something and I stepped out over John P's prone body though I wanted badly to kick him upright or to stamp on him and scream at him to get up to fuck and do this thing himself and I walked forward and forward and took aim at the centre of the boy's forehead though my hand was violently shaking and my aim was somehow true and that for a finish quietened him. Thanks be to God, I heard one of the Brien Cutters say behind me. I'm not sure to this day which one. I hardly spoke again beyond a line or two about the weather all down the years after to either of them, nor to Martin or Pat, my noble friends, my brothers in blood.

There are moments in days when I feel a swelling of something like pride, unbidden, unwelcome in my breast. Then I check myself. That I gave the command to aim and fire, that I alone stepped forward from the line, suspecting from the kick and heat from my weapon that my rounds were live and deadly, and despatched the boy when things fell to such bloody chaos, and despatched with him any sliver of a chance I might have had of solace in the stony future, is no reason to allow myself to ascribe any virtue to my actions. My blood was hot but I murdered him fair coldly. He was shackled and bound and helpless, beaten and soiled and begging. He was the son of a mother and a father and the child of a family and they're wondering about him yet.

I feel the closeness now of my end. I fell asleep in this chair the other evening and I woke of a sudden and the flickering television was gone and that whole end wall of the day room was bathed in light and all my blank-faced comrades were gone, replaced with a rank of winged creatures, at once transparent and solid, real and unreal, and at the centre of this apparition was a staircase of shimmering gold, and I wanted to raise myself and walk to it and put my foot on the first riser and look up to see could I know from the bottom what lay waiting at the top, but I found myself unable to move. I feel the breath on my forehead of an admonishing god. Or a finger-wagging saint at least, with plenipotentiary discretion. I'll be stopped for sure at the summit of those stairs, if I ever have the strength to climb them, and told Go back, you must wait, you must atone, and I'll state my case that I've atoned enough, each day since our summary execution of that wild boy. I haven't had a moment's ease since, not even in my hard-got sleep.

We swaddled him in canvas and we buried him fine and deep and we swept and fixed the earth above his grave and scattered twigs and leaves across it so that it would appear undisturbed and we said no prayer over it only stood for a moment in a half-circle with our eyes cast down and filed back down that hillside to the van and once again into the cold arms of the waiting years.

There's a weighing scales in the tiny cubicle of a bathroom in my room and I step up onto it every morning before my ablutions so I can chart in my mind the disintegration of myself, my falling away to nothing, quarter-pound by quarter-pound, a bag of sucky sweets a day. I'm not afraid to die and leave this place of sinners and sinned-against, guilty and innocent, and they all enmeshed and melded so no one is without stain, where only the faces of infant children are cast unsullied on the world, their only sin being done long ago by imaginary people in the pages of a book written by ancient men. I'm not even afraid or sad to leave my dear John P alone here because he'll know next to nothing of my passing and what sense he might have of an empty place beside him where once I sat will fade from him like a ghost in sunlight.

No good came of it. That's the miserable honest truth of it. John P's daughter never emerged from her silence, only pulled it more and more tightly around herself until it suffocated her, and her body was never got from the roiling sea. Her neatly folded note had only one word on it: Sorry. Her car was parked tidily in a corner of the car-park across the road from the climbing walk to the cliffs. It had a ticket on the dashboard to show she had paid as much for parking as the machine would allow her. The first three hours of her eternity were covered.

I know something of the bite and sting of the despair that led John P's daughter along that rising path at Moher. The notion overtook me shortly after it was all done that, having taken a life, I had in some way forfeited my own. I would breathe, but each breath would increase the debt I owed the universe. I felt myself undeserving of my happy, healthy children, brimming with goodness and love, and I think now looking back I in some way set about sabotaging things; it seems for all the world now as though I dismantled myself as surely as did that lovely girl. She flung and dashed herself to pieces in a few short moments; I did the same over long years, in a way as quietly violent. My son and daughter drag themselves in here to look at me the odd evening and it's as though they hate me: they huff and sigh and roll their eyes and pretend it's their restless children they're vexed with, and not me, not the memory of my tensed-up silent stewardship of the best part of their teenage years.

I fell into wickedness. I'd lose my reason over the tiniest of things: a murmur during the news; a clack and scrape of cutlery on a plate; a room not tightened to my liking. When they took to going out to discos I terrorized them. I harped and roared, and ridiculed my daughter's frocks and tops and my son's scraggy hair and torn trousers, and drove them everywhere even though they asked could they go on the bus with their pals and I'd sit outside and wait and bore holes in the walls of those places with my stares and I'd look in from the vestibule and their pals would see me and point and snigger and a time or two I marched in and enforced a distance between my daughter and a lad who looked as though he might be throwing shapes. My wife couldn't understand it at first. What in the name of God has got into you? But soon my crossness became the way of things and she wrung her hands and shook her head and lived with it for thirty years.

John P cast himself into silence as surely as his bruised and wingless angel cast herself into the sea. It was as though he took the mantle of it from her. His wife withered and died and it seemed as though her fading and passing made no odds to him. And I felt only gratitude for his wordlessness: there was safety in it, and a measure of comfort. It was no bother at all to me to call to him after. Isn't that strange, the ways of things, the ways of human minds? Once all our impecunious bargains had been done, I was free from my previous fear and unease and able again to cross my friend's threshold and sit and chat of weather and sport and news and local intrigues and watch him watching out the window for something, something, I don't know what. All old talk. Listening and nodding and watching. All of naught, to naught, for naught, year upon year of moments, of time slowly marked, of silence filled with empty words.

I often saw the outline of the boy after in the shapes of things living and dead, his head bowed, his body still tied fast, leaning forward from the filthy beam. In the gloaming especially, when spectres are born of shadows, in a tree in need of coppicing, say, or in a windblown fence, or in among a huddle of bulrushes. Some days in the mirror, looking at my monstrously normal face, I'd see reflected in the black parts of my eyes that ghostly post and its weight of torn flesh and shattered bones. And always those times a scream would rise in me and my blood would run to ice and my heart would spasm and pound.

I thought often of deserts in those wintry days, of walking into emptiness until my legs would carry me no further, of lying flat beneath a flaying sun, the flesh being cleansed from my bones, and they in turn being bleached white and dried to powder. That would be the death and disposal of my choosing, if I were able to grant myself the privilege of choice.

But here I am existing still.

Nephthys and the Lark

SHE COULDN'T SLEEP past dawn for the sound of wind. It seemed always to funnel down this road, pressed to wild gusts between the rows of houses. She imagined the roof being lifted by the eaves or a felled oak smashing through the rafters. But there was no oak near them, no trees at all, only clematis bushes and half-hearted hedges and puny garden willows. They could hardly claim treehood, drippy things. Her husband always said he loved the howl of a storm and the rain battering off the window glass. It made him feel cosy, he said, to be in out of it, in a warm bed. And there was a contentment to his snores, for sure, as though the raging weather really did lull him deeper into peacefulness. She considered hanging a foot out the side of the bed and, when it was cold enough, pressing it against his lower back where his pyjama top always rode up, but she wasn't sure she was still dextrous enough to pull it off. And she wasn't sure she was wicked enough to wake him that way.

A familiar chirruping filled the spaces between gusts. February the skylark's song always started. She'd been hearing him all week and she'd seen him skimming low across the green, landing on the edge of the rockery at its centre as she drove from the estate the morning before. She knew him by his raised plume, his rocker's coif, like it was gelled to standing. The cut of a young fella going to a disco. The sound of him, and the thought of his little hairdo, and the idea of the cold-foot trick, and the roar her husband would let out of him, and the laugh that would be in his *feck off* combined to a warmth in her stomach, a childish thrill of pleasures. The wind eased with the brightening of the sky, and she lay still, happy almost, for the hour before the alarm, waiting for the grunting and scratching of her husband's rising, his sighs and hums, the bellows and squeals of teenagers, the clomps and rattles of a waking house.

She told her three children they were having porridge. The youngest wanted to know why she'd bought Coco Pops if they weren't allowed to eat them. They were snuck into my trolley, she told him, and it won't be let happen again. You can have porridge with honey in it or you can go to school hungry. She leant and kissed the top of his sulky head and he winced and rubbed his hand along his crown. Ugh, Mamm-*y*. Her eldest boy had a hurley on his lap and he and his father were inspecting a crack along its bas, their foreheads almost touching. Her daughter was wearing makeup on her eyes and a skim of lipstick; her skirt was too far above her knees but she was wearing thick tights and it didn't seem worth the row. Her daughter had her iPhone in one hand and a slice of toast in the other and she was scrolling slowly with her thumb and chewing rhythmically, her eyes fixed to the little screen, the light of it reflected in them. The rain was gone and the wind had lost heart. A rainbow rose from behind the distant hills and arched across a sky of baby blue.

Her husband took the hurley and left it leaning against the back door, the way he'd remember to bring it as he passed out to his car. Jimmy Ryan will hoop that no bother, he told the boy. You can probably collect it on the way back from college. I'll text you and let you know. Sound, Dad. Her husband always had a redness in his cheeks in the mornings, and his thick hair clumped boyishly. He always showered and dressed after his breakfast, because he said he didn't like to go to work with a smell of food off him. He always took off his pyjamas and put on shorts and a T-shirt before he came downstairs, though, and a pair of flip-flops. He only ever got cross these mornings over those flip-flops. Where the *fuck* are my flip-flops? Pounding up- and downstairs, in and out of rooms. And the girl would roll her eyes and the boys would giggle and skit and she'd tell him to mind his language and they were in whatever corner he'd kicked them into the day before and she had more to be doing than minding his blessed flip-flops. A fifty-year-old man that can't mind one pair of flip-flops. I'm forty-nine. Not for long more, she'd say teasing, but she'd smile her best smile at him, because she knew it bothered him, the thought of turning fifty.

He was a buildings manager at a commercial complex. He worried non-stop. About cracks in plaster, moss in gutters, overloaded circuits, rising damp, descending wires. He found it hard to delegate. He had people under him but you wouldn't think it. You'd think he alone was holding up every building inside in that blessed complex, like Atlas holding up the world. She worried about him, the redness in his handsome face, the deepening creases at the sides of his eyes, the shots of blood in the whites of them; it couldn't be good for a man his age. Fretting about bricks and mortar. Those buildings would be standing a long time after him. At least he always slept well. Sleep is important. Her own eyes felt a bit gritty. The hours she'd lost to the moaning wind.

The youngest lad wouldn't give her a kiss at the school gate any more. He was nearly out of the car before it was fully stopped. First year in secondary was tricky. She wouldn't force the issue or embarrass him opposite his pals. But still it stung a little each morning. It pained her, the leaving go of that part of their relationship. The kisses would come back, she knew, when he was older, but they'd be manly, dutiful, perfunctory. The eldest was starting to do that now: he'd kissed her on the cheek last summer before going off on a holiday with his hurling team.

She'd heard one of the other lads saying something like Ooh, did you give your mammy a *kiss*? And he'd said something back like, I did, ya. Will I give yours a kiss as well? And that quietened the smart-arse, and she felt a burning pride in her son, and tears pinpricked the backs of her eyes. He was so like his father. He was already so much a man.

Her daughter had a boyfriend. A lad from town. Sixteen was too young for seriousness, but it was there. It was hard to talk to her. It was hard to think of her being pressured, feeling obliged, giving herself away too early, letting herself be used and cast away, letting her little heart get smashed to smithereens. There was no avoiding that pain, it seemed, no way of protecting her from it. Her daughter's world seemed compressed sometimes into the screen of that telephone; all of her tides turned at the pull of its gravity, her whole existence seemed wedded to it. She'd told her daughter to bring the boyfriend out home, but she hadn't yet. She was desperate for a proper look at him, to listen to his voice, to know if he was respectable, or respectful at least.

She stopped on the way back from town at the church. The car-park was low, surfaced in gravel; loughs of water lay along it. Rain often opened holes in the soft ground of it that would lie in wait for car-wheels beneath the treacherous puddles. She tutted and parked on the kerb, at the side of the main road, annoyed. Because the funds were there for the tarmacking, they'd been raised and left as yet unused. She'd helped with the fundraising herself, months ago, pushing alms envelopes through letter-boxes, selling books of tickets for raffles and lines for a sponsored fun-run. And her car was just out of tax, and she didn't want any nosy-parkers scanning her expired disc and thinking things that weren't true. She nearly drove away again, but she thought of a debt she owed to Saint Anthony from the previous week when the miraculous medal her grandmother had given her had gone missing. She'd promised to light candles, two euros a go, and the number of promised candles had increased from five to ten before she'd found the medal, sitting dusted with flour in the bowl of the weighing scales. She had the coins in her bag and the debt was being called in, softly but insistently, a whispered voice at the back of her mind.

She should have gone to the gym. She was after missing her spin class two weeks in a row. But the instructor had changed and she wasn't as happy with the new lad. He was very young-looking and his shout was a bit too screechy. And they'd upped the price to twelve euros for the hour from ten for those that hadn't paid the lot up front. All the smart ones paid in the one go, or the ones with the biggest arses anyway. They thought that'd surely force them into going every week, the idea of not getting what they'd paid for. She resolved to walk the block before work, once she had the vegetables done and the meat left out for the dinner, and the note of instructions for her husband written out and left stuck to the fridge. She settled her debt and said a few prayers and sat for a while not thinking of anything, her eyes focused on Our Lord in his agony. She was roused from her gentle reverie by a movement from the front pew; an old one making shapes to leave. She left herself before she was sucked into anything, gossip or small-talk, or the feeling of being judged, somehow, or of being made to feel unentitled to the company of Christ.

She peeled potatoes and chopped carrots and parsnips and left them in saucepans of water on the hob, ready. She took a sirloin joint from the fridge and dressed it in a casserole dish with onions and apple slices and covered it and slid it back into the fridge. She wrote on the back of an ESB envelope:

> 1. Turn on oven to 180. 2. When red light goes off put in meat from fridge. It should take two hours. 3. Drain

off juice and mix with OXO cube and water for gravy.
4. Turn spuds and vegetables on about 20 mins b4 meat cooked.

He knew what to do but still she always left the note, fastened to the fridge door with a magnet in the shape of the Eiffel Tower that the eldest boy had brought back from a school tour for her. She put on her tracksuit and walked the block fast, watching the hedgerows and gardens and greens for her lark, her little man. There was no sight of him, but she heard him again, thrilling, chirruping, pleading for love. She was flushed returning, her calves ached a little, but she felt good. Her morning had gone well and she had a bit of time left before her two to ten shift, so she could go easy with her shower, and she sang as she climbed the stairs, and thought of the weekend away she was going to surprise her husband with for his fiftieth, and the things she could do to take his mind off the march of his years.

The day room was empty when she arrived. The supervisor had them all in doing make-and-do in the arts and crafts room. The supervisor had a course done on that kind of thing, and she thought she was awfully swanky with the certificate they'd given her. It was framed on the wall of the arts and crafts room and it hung there like an accusation. Are you qualified to be in here, showing these people how to glue a button to a toilet roll? You are in your arse. You haven't a *certificate*. Anyway, how's ever. The supervisor was giving out yards about paint that was after being spilt on the floor and the spiller was standing bent-backed in contrition, one arm slung over his head, one still daubing at nothing with a dripping paintbrush. Sit *down*, sit *down* will you, the supervisor was saying, but the spiller wasn't stirring, and the supervisor's voice was getting louder, and her face redder, as she sopped at the bright blue puddle with a dirty-looking rag.

She was glad to be able to back out from there again, the mess of it; she was rostered onto the bungalow for the evening, where there were three profoundly handicapped patients, relatively elderly, mute, usually docile enough. There was a short walk from the main building's back door to the low bungalow flanked by trellised gardens and copses of young fruit trees. She felt the rising wind as she walked along the narrow path; she looked at the darkening sky. She hoped it wasn't going to turn stormy again. She'd forgotten to listen to the weather forecast. She'd Google it from the bungalow. She saw the new girl through the living-room window, standing with her hands at either side of her head. She was met at the bungalow door by screams. The new girl brushed past her, head down, almost charging. Thank God that day is over. The three of them are as quare all day. I don't know. I've notes left on the table. Good luck.

> Notes. Barry did pee at 12.10. No poo. He needs to go tho. Holding it. Mary L on console all day, gaga from it, wouldn't eat lunch. Mary M like a bitch. Scratching. Nails too long. Have told Nurse about Barry's no poo.

She breathed deeply, twice, three times, to steady herself. She clenched and unclenched her fists. She brought her hands together beneath her chin, tucking her elbows in tight to centre herself, like the yoga girl had said to do the time in the gym. She ignored Barry's wails from the corner of the room where he was clutching his bum with one hand and describing wild arcs in the air with the other and walked to the giant bean-bag where Mary L sat, the flickering light of her child's game console reflected in her wide brown eyes. Mary L. Mary L. Look at me. You have to put away that a minute and eat your food. Mary L. Mary L. And she reached down with her left hand and closed it around the top of the grey plastic console and as Mary L looked up she drew her right hand behind her and swung it back across Mary L's cheek with just a shade short of all her strength. Mary L tumbled sideways from the bean-bag onto the floor, and lay there, long keening sobs escaping her. She took a handful of the hair at the back of Mary L's head and entwined it in her fingers, and yanked upwards, so that Mary L screamed shrilly at the shocking pain, and rose to all fours, and she pulled on the hair so that Mary L began to crawl forward to lessen the pressure and relieve the pain, and in that way she was able to get Mary L across the living area and up onto a chair, and she took a segment of the sandwich that had been prepared earlier that day by the new girl and as a long wail exited Mary L's mouth the sandwich entered it, and Mary L's eyes bulged, and she bucked and coughed, and her hands went up towards her face but they were batted back down and the bread and ham and grated cheese fell in wet clumps from her mouth to the table and her lap.

Eat. The fucking. Sandwich. Mary L, eat it. Eat it. And she gathered the spit-covered clumps in a square of kitchen paper and smashed them back in past Mary L's cracked lips and through the gaps in her teeth, and pushed upwards with one palm from beneath her chin and downwards with the other on the top of her head, so that Mary L could breathe only through her nose, and the air that was rushing in and out through her nostrils sent flailing lines of watery snot outwards and down, along her chin, and Mary L clawed at the arms and the hands that were holding her mouth closed, but it was no good, and all she could do was swallow, because she knew that's what she was supposed to do, and then this would end.

Mary M and Barry were quiet now, watching. Barry was still holding his bum. She wiped Mary L's face, and kissed her cheek, and said Good girl, Mary L, now look at you, aren't you the great girl to eat your lunch after all, and they all saying you're only a bad bitch? You're not at all, you're a great girl, so you are. Eat up the rest of it now. And she walked around the table and over to the kitchen area where she ran hot water over her hands and scrubbed them with anti-bacterial soap, and dried them slowly, her eyes meeting Barry's all the while. He knew. He pointed towards the toilet door, and raised his eyebrows. Yes, Barry, she said. Get in there right now and do your poo, or I'll fucking kick it out of you. Get in, you little bastard, and shit. And you can wipe your own arse. Mary M, sit down on your seat and watch your DVDs and mind your own fucking business.

And that way the evening was set, and everyone knew to be quiet and good, and it was not too bad, and she was able to Google the weather forecast, and watch *Emmerdale*, and *Corrie*, and they ate nearly all of the fish-fingers and waffles and beans that were delivered from the kitchen, and the nurse came in around eight with the tablets, and she passed no remark on Mary L's livid cheek, and after the second *Corrie* the three put on their jim-jams no bother and toddled off to their beds.

The air was clear and still as she drove home, the low-pressure front had moved away. There were stars winking down from the gaps between clouds. She hoped her husband had cooked the meat properly. She hoped he hadn't had a stressful day. She hoped in the morning she'd hear the skylark sing.

Sky

THE ROAD OUTSIDE this house is the same one my mother and father walked together each morning of their married life to Mass. Hand in hand, then arm in arm as they got older. That now is nearly seen as being sinful. Daily Mass-going is a thing to be suspicious of. Have you nothing better to be doing? No, faith, I have not. It's not as though I sink too deeply into it; I only do it in memory of my dear parents. I only stay on nodding terms with Christ, just in case. What harm can it do to send a prayer or two skyward?

Suspicious also is living where you were born, on the road your parents walked. Did you never want to have a look at the world? No, faith, I did not. This road is as good as any, or as bad. The crows that blacken the sky above my yard each night are descended from the ones my mother watched. The same squawks and caws in the same prickled sky. What business have those crows in the hills east of here? Something important takes them there with each dawn, anyway, to Pallasbeg and Pallasmore and Ton Temma. They process home with the fading light, an hour or so of staggered returning, weighed down and weary. And I stand beneath them, wondering, the way my mother and father did.

Crows have great notions. They perch before bed for a nightly confab on the ridges of the roofs of all this town's important buildings: the courthouse and the town hall and the bank. They never grace the grocery shops or townhouses or any of the lesser structures, only relieve themselves on them as they pass.

Then they shout across at one another all the news of the day. There's three gangs, as far as I can make out, with a HQ each, triangled around the square, shouting over Our Lord's stony grey head. Three factions, one murder. Once they've all their arguing and organizing done they turn their arses to the town and peel away to the dark insides of the giant evergreens in the grounds of the two Saint Marys. They're fixed as firm to their home as I am to mine.

The houses of this road are strung with sorrow, like rows of old houses anywhere. A map of loss plotted all down it. Children taken, a preponderance of boys, accidents and sickness and other things. All those people would presume the stab of their sorrow to be unknown to me, occluded from me, but they're wrong. I well know the freezing grip of it, the way it can steal the breath from your lungs, the jagged thumping of a broken heart.

I saw a light like a moving star one night in early winter. Right the way from east to west it floated and it was back again a while later, and hurled itself across the vaulted sky in two or three short minutes. My neighbour told me it was the International Space Station, orbiting the Earth, and there was men and women inside in it. He was out watching it too. He'd heard on the radio it was going to be clearly visible that night. Spacemen and spacewomen, flying in a space station. What separated them from me? The line of the sight of my eye, nothing, everything. I've seen that speeding light since, a good few times, and others like it. Satellites, my neighbour said, and he even knew the names of some of them. I started reading up on science after seeing that spacecraft, in books and magazines, at the library mostly, and I learnt a lot about things. The names of the parts of the heavens known to man and visible to man's naked eye. I read about the Very Big and the Very Small and how there's nothing to bind the two but the ideas of mankind, his fistful of imaginary strings. What things are made of, the particles of us.

My sister's child was named after my father, as I was. William. I always called him Billy, as I never was. He was as good as reared in this house because my sister was leaving her husband for most of the years of his childhood. A slow departure, a long and gently sloped vale of tears. My mother and father hardly once took their eyes off of him. Then they departed this world nearly as one when little Billy was only barely four and I wasn't long turned thirty and it was hard for me to tell him where they'd gone. So I pointed at the sky at night and told him they were winking down at him from there and he seemed happy enough with that. My sister was more settled in herself by then and her husband had gone abroad somewhere and she took to doing college courses and bettering herself and I was always here waiting at the gate for Billy, for nights and weekends and weeks at a time. And I'd make him scrambled eggs and sausages in the mornings and look at cartoons with him warm and sleepy on top of me on the couch and take him to the park and the pictures and the swimming pool. And I'd stand at his bedroom door at night and look at him and listen to his breaths. And I'd kiss him on the cheek and wet his hair with tears as he left and I held him to me once until he wriggled free of me and one morning shortly after a letter came in a light blue envelope and it was from my sister and it was to tell me Billy wouldn't be visiting for a while because he had to study for his summer tests and he had hurling training twice or three times a week now and he'd have adventure camp all summer and they'd see me probably before Christmas.

That Christmas came and went without a sign of them or word from them and as spring neared and a fierce longing had grown inside in me for just a look at Billy, for a day with him, for an afternoon even, or an hour of the sound and sight and nearness of him, I wrote a letter to Lourda and a reply came shortly after declaring that there was good news and more good news: she had met a lovely man and he wanted to set up home with her in England and Billy was so fond of him and he so fond of Billy and they wouldn't be tormenting me any more because Lourda had her master's degree got now and the promise of academic work in an English university and after I had all that good news read and read again I made a cup of tea and set it on the kitchen table before me and sat down to watch the sun disappear behind the Arra Mountains and I was still sitting looking out at the sky as it reddened with the same sun's rising and my tea was cold, undrank before me.

My Billy is well into his manhood now and I haven't seen him since that last embrace.

There's a man walks up and down this road most days with makeup smeared and daubed onto his face and a string of pearls across his bared and hairy chest. He has several of the signs of the zodiac fandangled from his blue-veined earlobes. He never talks to me nor would I want him to except the once he stopped outside my gate and asked had I the loan of a tenner because he was fierce stuck for a box of fags. I told him I hadn't it and he asked had I a fiver so. And again I shook my head and he hawked and spat on the path outside my gate and stomped off towards the corner in a pair of dirty runners with his ruffled skirt swishing around his pale and knotted calves. And I envied him, I'm not really sure why. The freedom he'd granted himself, maybe, to be only missing a smoke.

I rang a number one time I read off of the notice board in the vestibule of the church. I didn't mean to memorize it, but my eye was drawn to it so often, and the picture underneath it in black and white of a woman with a hand across her forehead and a phone to her ear and her long hair drawn across her face, and an air about her of sadness and need, that it sat as clear as day before my mind's eye. Then I felt a terrible rush of embarrassment when a girl answered, with a lovely soft voice, kind and warm. She asked me my name and I said William and regretted not having had a lie ready. I started to tell her how I missed my little nephew and then remembered he was only little now in my memory of him; wherever he was he'd be a man, tall and good-looking and athletic, with only a vague memory of an auld uncle he used to be minded by now and again in his childhood. No matter what, I'll never see that little boy again. Does the man who was the boy think of me? Hardly if at all, I'd say. I'm only a ghost to him now, and he a ghost to me.

I hung up all of a shot for a finish, barely having mumbled my thanks to the girl who was trained to give sympathy, and sat on the seat at the telephone table in the hall in a stew of embarrassment, and a shame, at once strange and familiar, that rose from somewhere, I don't know, I don't know where.

That wasn't the finish of my foolishness, though. I fell back into it not even a year later. I read a number that appeared on the television at the end of a programme that was about finding lost family. As I listened to the foreign ringtone I imagined Billy might answer. That kind of a thing happens: wedding rings lost on beaches turning up years later in the bellies of fishes caught by the loser; identical twins separated at birth and never knowing one another turning out to have the same jobs and children of the same names. But it wasn't Billy, of course. I went off half cocked into my story to another soft-voiced girl, this one with a lovely English accent. Once I stopped talking, after telling her how the years without word from Lourda or Billy had stacked themselves one upon the other almost unknown to me into decades, she was silent a long moment until I said Hello, are you still there? I'm so sorry, William, she said, nearly in a whisper, but that's not really the type of scenario we're interested . . . and she caught herself and said instead, In a position to get involved in . . . it's more of a . . . a . . .

A what? I could have said. A *what*? I could have been sour with her, indignant. But I ended her discomfort, her struggle to parse my story into a single word by pushing down the contacts with my finger and I left the receiver cradled between my shoulder and chin and sat listening for a good long while to the unbroken bleep as my tears pooled between plastic and flesh, thinking of heart monitors and hospice bedrooms, and souls unshackled from gravity.

I did a computer course in the library and I learnt how to look things up and about search terms and Googles and all of that. I searched there, and searched, and found nothing. The young lad who was the instructor helped me to send away online for a laptop computer of my own and he showed me how to get broadband for the house on a little square thing that only had to be plugged in and turned on and connected remotely.

When my laptop came I unpacked it and plugged it in and turned it on and connected it to the broadband step by step the way I'd learnt and I clicked on the Google symbol and the empty rectangular window came up with the cursor inside in it and I looked at it as it blinked and winked back at me and my heart palpitated in time with it and I got scared all of a sudden of what was in behind that window, and the lack of a watching instructor or librarian behind me, and the unfettered access to everything I now had, a world of knowledge and nonsense, and none of it any real use to me, and I unplugged the laptop and the broadband and put them in the back of the hall closet and they're in there still. And the money goes out of my account every month still without fail for the broadband.

The sky is enough for me, I decided, and the wonder of all

the things in it, besides concerning myself with the webs and ways of imaginary people. What knowledge is there, really? What can be known?

That silence can open between people that can become a gap, a distance, a gulf, and widen and deepen, and be for a finish fathomless and untraversable.

That the crows will leave one morning for their last day's work and I'll look one night at the sky above me for the last time and feel the cooling of the cores of distant galaxies.

That all things tend towards chaos, and chaos itself tends in its turn towards stillness and peace.

That all the parts of all the atoms and protons and quarks and leptons of the stars and of me and of the haughty crows and of my parents and of Lourda and of my Billy and all the things that are or ever were will arrange themselves for a finish equidistant from each other in all directions and stop still there in the darkness and the cold.

From a Starless Night

I PUT ON MY running gear this morning early and went downstairs and out the door and started to run. The landlord was smoking a fag outside his shop, facing away from me. I crossed the road to avoid talking to him. Murty is sound but I knew he was waiting there for news, for the story. I couldn't face it. His shop-girls would have told him there was something up. They'd have seen the leaving through the window yesterday, the comedy of boxes and baling twine.

I went slowly at first. Under the birdsong, through the fumeless breeze, past the Lidl that was once the Davin Arms where we'd meet and pretend to be strangers; past the deathly whitewashed front of Ivan's where we used to go to buy posh bread and wine; past the tyre place and the garage and the Limerick Inn hotel where I used to work weekends washing dishes when we were in college and she'd always ring me when the kitchen hummed the most and all the chefs would roll their bleary eyes and chop and clang harder in temper; past the roundabouts and traffic lights and onto the shoulder of the motorway, into the clean and still and misty countryside, into the morning, the rising day.

Jenny told me the night before last that I was disconnected. We gave until the sunrise to exchanging sentences starting with *I'm the one* and *You're the one*. I begged her but she told me all my chances were used up. Her father came to collect her yesterday morning. She left the flat bare behind her save for a hillock of tat, summited by the ornamental Ganesh that I bought for her in New Delhi. There's an echo now that was never there before; all the soft, downy things are gone, there's nothing to swallow the sounds of me. I sat on the edge of a kitchen chair in the middle of my plucked flat and blew smoke in Ganesh's elephant face and said, Well, Ganesh, what the fuck will we do now? And he said nothing back, only sat four-armed and cross-legged and stared at me through his alabaster eyes.

I don't like being alone in the flat. I saw a ghost one time, walking across the kitchen floor from right to left. She was wearing jeans and a long, loose shirt; her hair was long and brown, her face was pale. She lived there once, and was killed in a car crash. She was coming home, she didn't know she was dead. I never told Jenny; it happened on a weekend night. She hardly ever stayed in the flat on weekends, she stayed in the habits of college: going home Friday evenings to her family and childhood friends, bussing it back late Sunday or early Monday. Murty's wife called a priest she knew and he came one day when we were at work and anointed the walls and floors and whispered gently to the dead girl to walk into the light. I think she did; I haven't seen her since. I'm still afraid she'll come back, though, and frighten the piss out of me again.

Anyway, I am alone, and there doesn't seem much I can do about it. I texted Jenny a few times but she hasn't replied. Or I don't think she has: the keys on my phone are frozen. She's gone from me. I'm not sure exactly why, but it's got something to do with coldness, with absence, with non-engagement. Things like that. I didn't see this coming, though, her sudden burst of temper and tears, this exodus.

This is it, so, she said, and smiled with her lips downturned so her chin dimpled sweetly. I felt, I felt. Something new. A concentrated kind of love for her, winding me. A knowing that she wasn't coming back. Will you be okay? Ya, ya, I'll be grand, I said, in a whisper. She said, Hug? I just stood there so she walked over to me and put her arms around me and I stood stiff and unmoving though I hadn't planned on being sulky and she drew away saying Oh for fuck's sake in a weary voice and she was gone down the stairs before I looked up from the naked floor.

Her father crammed his ancient Jetta with her stuff and his big hand swallowed mine and he pumped it up and down just once and leaned in close to me and his forested nostrils flared and he jerked his head sideways towards his idling car and tear-streaked daughter and said, There's plenty more fish in the sea, son. She's as contrary as they come, anyway, that one. And he looked over at her, a gleam of adoration in his eyes, and he tied the lock of his boot to his tow-bar with a length of baling twine, and they were gone.

I ASKED MY mother the same questions over and over when I was small. Why have I no granny and granddad? Why do we never go on our holidays? She'd answer, a different answer every time it seemed to me, and her words would make no sense to me. I'd know from a shimmer of change in the set of her face and a coldness that would enter her eyes when to stop. I knew her so completely, so deeply. I felt the changes in the air about her, I sensed her quickening temper, her softening, the tides of her. I was besotted, obsessed; I mooned about her, I constantly wanted to touch her, to press myself into her softness. Jesus Christ, will you get out from under my feet, she'd say, and I'd crawl behind the couch and cry, and she'd lift me out and say, Sorry, little darling, sorry, my little man. And we'd sleep on the couch, curled into each other, in the long and empty afternoons.

Once, when I was four or maybe five, I made a batch of

mud-men, in a wheelbarrow at the side of our house. I'd been crying over something and had lost myself in the making of them, limbless figures ranked in three files with hair of grass and features of tiny stones, and my mother said she loved them, my tiny army, they were gorgeous so they were, and so was I. She brushed my fringe back from my forehead and kissed the back of my head and my salt-stiff cheek, and I smelt fags off her, and perfume, and felt in that moment as though all the universe only existed so I could be there, beneath the sun, being kissed by her.

She's going out with a man the last few years who used to be a farmer until he sold half his land and set the other half. Any time I meet him he turns red and the hand he offers me shakes a bit, and I feel sorry for him. How's business? he asks. How's things in the computer world? The finest, I say, all go. I talk the way he does to settle him, to stop him being nervous. I'm not worth being nervous over. Good, begod, he says. That's the way to have it. Sure is, I say, and we look at each other, unsure of how to look away. Did you see the match? he asks me every time, and I lie that I did and he settles into a long analysis and the redness and uneasiness slowly recede. And I like that he's there, for her, so I can more easily be not there, for her.

My father's name was Finbar. I didn't always know he was my father. He was an old man when I was a child, but tall and handsome, and he lived in a bungalow halfway up the Long Hill. He wore dark suits and smoked non-stop. He'd had a wife one time who had died. There was a picture of her in the kitchen, smiling beside the Sacred Heart. I'd be dropped at his gate and he'd answer the door with an expression of surprise, and act as though his life was completed by the sight of me. He lived three streets and a lifetime away from my mother. She'd been his secretary once, for a few months, and something had happened that led to me. He built a room on the back of his house for me, with a skylight, so I could look at the stars as I fell asleep. But all I ever saw was plain blackness. Finbar would look up at the starless night and down at me and put his hand on my face and say Sleep tight, little man. And in the mornings he'd say Come on, little man, rise up out of it. He never took me anywhere. It was years before I realized he'd been ashamed; not of me, but of the fact of my existence.

Finbar died when I was eleven and a man told me in the living room of the bungalow as I sat and stared in wonder at the stillness and smokelessness of Finbar's corpse that he was my brother. He looked almost as old as Finbar had. He was bald and he wore glasses and his eyebrows were black and bushy and curled upwards at the ends like a cartoon devil but his face changed and seemed kind when he smiled. He told me he'd fallen out with Finbar years and years before and he'd never gotten the chance to make up with him. We had words, he said. Over you. Me? And he nodded, and then I knew, without anything more being said. Always be nice to your mother, he said. Don't ever fall out with her. Or if you do, be sure and make it up. And I never saw that man again that said he was my brother. But someone sold Finbar's house and my room at the back of it and I suppose it must have been him.

When I was fourteen I kicked a kitten against a wall with all my strength. I'd been walking through the castle demesne and saw her there, standing still, crying softly. There was a wet crack when the kitten struck the wall as tiny perfect pulsing things inside her burst. The day stopped, the breeze fell away, a drifting leaf came to rest at my feet. There was nothing now that could be done to undo this thing I'd done. I turned away and walked home and my mother asked how I was as I passed her in the hallway and I ignored her as I always did in those years but I wanted to cry and beg her to make it that I didn't kill the cat, to make the world rewind so the clenching thing inside me would loosen and fall away.

Jenny left me once before, but I knew that she'd come back that time. But just to feel our scales were balanced I went to town and walked up Pery Square and nodded at a dark-haired girl who stood with her back to the railings of the People's Park. There was glittery makeup on her face, her green-brown eyes were blackly ringed; her breath was warm and slightly sour, her teeth were prettily gapped. I told her what I wanted and I paid her twice what she asked for and she nodded and smiled and stroked me gently until I slept and kissed my ear to wake me in the early morning. I drove her back to town in the cold dawn and dropped her near a shabby door on a passage off a lightless street. I waited to see if she'd look back at me. But she didn't. What did I expect?

You can't destroy energy. So every sound ever made still exists. Everything I've ever said is still floating through the ether, and everything that was ever said to me. I stood before a whalebone in the natural history museum once that was set on a plinth behind a screen of glass and I imagined my father was standing beside me, a made-up father, young and lean, T-shirted and muscular. The two of us marvelled, and whistled our wonder; his arm lay lightly along my shoulders. I cried at the memory of a thing that never happened. Fuck you, Finbar, I said, out loud, but no one heard. And those words are floating gently still around the universe. I hope he never hears them.

I often wondered where my mother went the nights I was in Finbar's house. Maybe she was out, with friends, or men, being young, or maybe she just needed a break, to be alone, away for a while from my relentless love.

*

BUNRATTY WAS SUDDENLY behind me and I was only a downhill and an easy straight from Shannon. I wondered at my freshness, the lack of pain in my knees and ankles. I realigned my shoulders, hips and knees, and set my face to the cool breeze, and soon I was passing the empty guard box at the airport gate.

I saw a pilot on the edge of the wide path. He was smoking a cigarette, watching me approach, leaning against the metal jamb of the gate in the fence along the edge of the hangars for private jets. He was smiling at me. A black Gulfstream sat soaking sunlight on the concrete, parked at an angle from the nearest hangar, its nose cone cocked outwards almost jauntily, in a way that made it look as though it had been parked up in a hurry, like a car left on double yellows while an errand was being hastily run. I slowed to a walk as I neared him. He breathed a line of smoke skyward and said: Hello, friend. You look tired. Come and sit and have some coffee with me. And he ground his butt with a gleaming shoe and pushed himself away from his slouch and started to walk without looking back, and I followed him.

He showed me the controls of the jet, the throttle and the tiller pedals, the altimeter and trim counter and radar screen; he offered me his headpiece and his hat and roared with laughter when I put them on, and I looked across the tarmac at the distant terminal building and the viewing area where Mam and me sometimes used to go for a day out to watch the planes take off and land, and I was sure I could see two figures there looking back at me, a dark-haired man and a fair-haired child. I looked west at the glint from the water of the Shannon estuary where it lapped across the mudflats of Rineanna, and I thought how mad it was that I was here, with this sallow smiling man, and I took a small white cup of coffee from him that was haloed by wisps of steam, and he said that he was sad this day and he would tell me why.

His father had been a hotelier, a big man who laughed a lot and helped his neighbours with their problems. He turned to Mecca and prayed when he was meant to, but he was more observant than devout, a friend to all men. His father had been accused of harbouring insurgents and was taken one night and held for an autumn and winter in a prison at the edge of their town. Visits were not permitted. His father was released one cold morning and sent walking home barefoot. He was a different man, stooped, narrowed, yellowed, curled-up and dried to cracking like a fallen leaf. His eyes seemed wider in his shrunken face; they were cast down and filled with darkness. When he spoke, he addressed the ground, in a whisper, as though afraid his jailers would hear him, and take offence, and return for him. And he shrank and shrank from fear until nothing was left, and he slipped from this life without noise.

I told him in return about Finbar. Fin – bar, he said. Finbar. This is a nice name, the name of a kind man. We're sons of the same father, he said. We're brothers. And I noticed then a movement in a leather holdall that was sitting open on a jump-seat near the cockpit door, and a kitten poked its white head up and looked at me, and held my eye, and disappeared again into its nest. My new friend half closed the bag's top and whispered into the darkness of it: Sleep, little fellow.

He rose and beckoned to me to follow him through the cockpit door and he looked into my eyes and smiled sadly before drawing back a curtain that was closed across the plane's passenger area. Two men sat slumped on reclined seats, each turned to half face the other, their heads back, their throats cut. Blood was blackening on their shirts, their mouths were open in rictuses of shock, their eyes were mercifully closed. This one, the pilot said, pointing at the dead man on the left, this one is the man who lied about my father, and had him jailed, and ordered that he be starved and beaten. And this one, he said, pointing at the other dead man, was a captain in the army of liberation that came to my village and took from my family all the things needed for living.

The kitten swished suddenly past my legs and down the steps to the tarmac and disappeared. I followed it down without looking back and ran into the afternoon sun, back towards the city. I stopped at the top of my road and looked down towards the shop with our flat above it, Jenny's and mine, and remembered myself the way I used to be, before the thunderheads rolled in. I remembered sleep unscored by dreams of falling. I prised the key from the inside of my wristband and felt a burning where it had pressed against my flesh. I opened the wooden door and went upstairs and lay along the couch and slept, and woke in the evening, in the dying light, and saw Finbar, sitting in the armchair across from me. My runners were where I'd left them the night before, unworn, waiting. My gear was still draped on the wooden kitchen chair. My blood was darkening on the floor.

Come on, my father said. You're okay now. Rise up out of it, son, and I'll bring you home.

Hanora Ryan, 1998

THERE'S GOING TO be war, my father said one day in 1914. Inside in Nenagh. I spied all the bould Fenians pelting off down the hill from Barbaha this morning early. Off in to roar and bawl outside the door of the *Guardian* office. Up in arms over recruitment posters. Not a hand's turn done between them, I'd say. Lord but they must have great wives. There'll be war, says he, and he shaking his head. Mark that now, ye can. Let ye not go in gawking, now, let ye not. Stay well away from all that. There'll be lads taken to the barracks, as sure as God.

The *Nenagh Guardian* was that time owned and always was all along the years before by loyal subjects of their fragrant majesties beyond and Daddy said the likes of them was always minded like heifers in calf. It wasn't until a year or two later, 1916 I'm nearly sure, that the *Guardian* was bought by the Ryans who own it still to this day. (No relations of mine except like as not the way all Ryans are related if you go far enough back along the ages.)

I'll blister ye, Daddy said, if I hear of ye inside near the place. But I saw no crossness on his face as he turned away from my brothers and my sister and me, back to his foddering. As if such a thing was possible, that he'd have ever left a mark on one of his children. My gentle father, and he all about the war, the war.

The posters were torn down anyway and stamped into the mud and more were put up and the RIC ringed a man called Waxer Walsh and roped him and dragged him down Barrack

Street and a small band of Irish Volunteers went about springing him and a man was shot in the arm and that was the finish of the hoo-hah for a good long while. But any man who went about answering the call of king and country that was printed by the *Nenagh Guardian* on those posters and on the front page of their newspaper was told to expect no peace or place in the Tipperary they'd return to. They'd choke on the bread the king's shilling bought, and their families with them.

Robert Wesson Coleman was five or six years older than me. He gave many a day palling with us, only half in secret. He played hurling with my brothers above in the long acre and he showed them a rugby ball one time and their eyes widened in wonder. The quare shape of it. My sister was in love with him. I suppose I was too, but though I was younger I was less inclined to be fanciful or to be overtaken fully by such things the way Mary was. My eldest brother said he hated Rob Coleman because he was a dirty English land-robbing bastard but when we heard he'd fallen in Flanders Fields my brother went out to the barn and cried.

I read a poem years upon years later written by William Butler Yeats. Lord God it knocked the breath from my body and the words from my mind. It was about another Robert, though his name was not mentioned in the lines of the poem but in the explanation beneath, written by some professor of such things. Major Robert Gregory, the poem was presumed to be about, the son of Lady Gregory, and he for all the world by the sounds of it the very self-same as my Robert. A boy from a big house told he had a fealty and a duty to a foreign land by virtue of the blood in his body. The boy in the poem didn't hate his enemy nor love his king; Kiltartan was his country, the poor of that place his people. That's out there beyond Gort in County Galway. We went there for a spin one Sunday, and drove down into Coole Park to see the swans and the famous names carved into the trees. I got a terrible lonesome feeling. Your man Yeats couldn't have known the thoughts that were in that boy's head as he flew his fighter plane towards the heavens but my soul be damned if he was too far wrong.

There's many a family of this place and here around lost a son or a brother or a father but never could they raise a stone or a cross in their honour. Their memories were buried in silence and shame. The Colemans, being free to fight for England, could commission plinths and plaques from the best of masons and fix them firm to the earth. And why wouldn't they? Why wouldn't they do their damnedest to keep on to their dear Robert in some way, in cold stone and carved words.

One of the Donnells of Gortnabracken came back, shell-shocked and nearly deaf. He made no bones about where he'd been and would stand aside for no man, regardless of rank or station. He'd set his face to hell and hadn't flinched. But still and all he'd be silent for weeks and months at a time, hunched and white, then all of a sudden he'd be shouting and roaring around the pubs and streets, standing and kneeling at the wrong times in Mass and saying his prayers too loud and laughing, thinking the rest of the world was gone the same way as him. His brothers did their level best to quieten him, and his parents were warned by the Volunteers who by then had become the IRA to keep a rein on him; Father Fitzwilliam even beseeched from the pulpit on his behalf. The sacrifice he made, what he gave of himself; fighting in a just war blessed by God, and his right mind left behind him in Passchendaele.

I heard that boy of the Donnells – what's this his first name was? – say more than once how there was a good many men of his battalion shot for not wearing their hats opposite officers or not saluting them properly or for other such niggardly transgressions.

The Irish lads were dirt to them, nothing, not even human. Men that left this parish and ones like it, imagine, decent poor men that took themselves away from these green fields and rolling hills, to fight against a Kaiser for a king, were shot by little jumped-up Johnny Englishmen for not having their uniforms on properly, or for falling asleep, or for not lepping quick enough over the tops of trenches into the teeth of death. He was sent off for a finish to live with an old uncle that was left a childless widower above in Templetuohy. I heard he began drilling young lads up there for the IRA and that he blew himself to smithereens trying to make a barrel-bomb to roll out onto the road in front of a truckload of Black and Tans.

There wasn't a coffin to be got here, you know, for a full year once that First World War ended. The Spanish flu was brought back by soldiers, and laid waste to all about. All the weak were taken: babies and old people and anyone already disposed to frailty or sickness. And many a strong man and woman that was never sick a day in their lives. No resistance, you see, it blew through them the very same as the wind through the girders of the railway bridge between Ballina and Killaloe. I clearly remember the day of my seventeenth birthday, going on the trap with my father to town, and seeing a line of coffins at the bottom of Queen Street, and another row started where that one ended, of poor souls shrouded in blankets and sheets, rosary beads draped across their breasts. And the Foleys in the sawmill yard working night and day to provide short planks for makeshift coffins, and the priests and the curates stepping along the ranks of dead, anointing them. The stench, I'll never forget, of rotting things and incense. The hums and chants of prayers, the wailing cries.

I heard a man say years upon years later on a television programme that that was all needed by humankind, all that death.

It was Nature's way of pruning back excess, of ensuring bounty. That was needed, says he. The world was short of orphans. The earth was short of human flesh and bones. Lord, but isn't it a sight altogether the things people say, the things they think they know, the certainties they carry about for themselves. As full as ticks with satisfaction at their own smartness.

I'll die soon, I suppose. I'll hardly get a look at this new millennium that all the hullabaloo is about. The world will go haywire by all accounts, the minute it turns 2000. Machines will all turn off, or go quare on people, or something. I'm as well off out of it if that's the case. Robert Coleman is eighty years dead, imagine. That beautiful boy from the big house who walked many a summer day along the far bank of the stream that served as a border between my father's tiny freehold and his father's estate of two or three thousand acres. Who talked and laughed across the whispering water, and always waved back at me as he started up the hill towards home.

The House of the Big Small Ones

TRUE AS GOD. True as this pint before me. I told Busty McGrane go fuck herself. Straight into her face I told her. Years ago this was when all they had was the pub and the little shop counter at the front of it and only the bare bit of milk and bread and ham and newspapers being sold there that time and even only scarcely that. Before the big swanky Mace come along and the yard full of pumps under a canopy. Only the one lonesome pump that time and no diesel even. Farmers only used diesel them days anyway and all had their own tanks. I was only a puck, sixteen or seventeen. Says to myself Right, I'll set out early on for this cow how things is going to be between us. Few hundred pound them days a man could be in Australia and all set up. Didn't need no job at all off of that wan. Was me doing her the favour.

So there we was on a Sunday evening fine and sunny and a thirst in my throat like sandpaper was rubbing the inside of it and it a bank holiday Monday next day and Mickey Briars and Alphonsus Reilly and all them lads that was all off the next day shouting over at me from inside in Ciss Brien's that I was only a boy, a bare chap for that orange crowd, and wanting to know was I a fuckin gom altogether or what was I and Busty McGrane standing before me reading me from a height over the dust in the yard and it being rose good-oh by every passing car and truck and destroying her windows and all the stuff inside in the shop was covered entirely in grit. Hers was the only shop in the country them days opened Sundays. And there I stood and her two tits heaving up and down before me while she screeched, mesmerizing me. How am I meant to keep dust from rising, I asked her. Hose it down, says she, and the screech of her near split me in two. Piss on it for all I care! And she poked a long finger into my chest. Well, if she did! Says I to myself, I can die a man or live a child, and I turned around to her and *lifted* her out of it. Busty, says I – and that alone, calling her Busty and not Mrs McGrane fair vexed her – says I, Go on. Away. And fuck. Yourself. Real slow, like that, straight into her face. And I thrown down my sweeping brush and strolled fine and slow with no look back away from her across to Ciss's, her main competition as things were then, and was landed up a pint straight the second I walked through the door in congratulations though I wasn't even strictly of age, but then you're only a man when you start to act like a man. True as God I done that. And she never once barked at me since. Not like all them young wans she'd have shitting themselves scared of her, doing their few hours for their bit of pocket money, handing out cones to children and standing idle at the tills looking out of their mouths. True as God. Ask Mickey Briars if you don't believe me.

Then a small while after, and I having the ticket as good as got to go over to Australia and work in demolition with the father's cousin, didn't one of the young Comerfords land down to our cottage saying how I was wanted inside in The House of the Big Small Ones. Philomena McGrane was after telephoning their house with the message on account of we had no phone of our own that time, and my father says to me More in your line now to go in as far as the village and make it up with the McGranes and get back your bit of a job and don't mind your fooling about Australia or what have you. Imagine the cut of you, says he, you'd be sizzled like a rasher and swallowed whole by a crocodile for his breakfast on your first day off of the plane. And

I kind of seen the sense in that then, that when a man is offered a good job in the place of his birth isn't it as well take his luck where it comes besides travelling to ungodly places looking for what you're only after leaving behind you. And so in I went and the auld husband inside in the bar and it dark as night inside in it as always and it still called The House of the Big Small Ones that time on account of the measures was always gave out massive all along the years before the McGranes blew down from the north and bought it off of auld Mugsy Foley and he half dead that time and no son or daughter left to look after him and the auld wife long buried and he desperate stuck for the few pound to put himself up in the good home out beyond Lackanavea not to be ended up below in the county home that was always along the years known as The Poorhouse. And the auld husband had a puss on him and all he done was grunt at me and nod towards the door behind the bar in towards the kitchen where Busty sat keeping a watch out on shop counter and bar counter and petrol pump and husband.

Look on, says she, in the auld nordie accent, and a big long fag in her hand and a halo of smoke about her head. Look what the cat's dragged in. Kee-at, says she, like that, in place of cat. Them auld nordies do always make words longer and split them in two. Are you over your little strop, says she, like for all the world I was a bould schoolboy waiting to see would he be slapped or gave out to or both or neither. I said nothing back to her only stood my ground and done my damnedest not to be leaving my eyes settle of their own accord on the front of her tight pink jumper. She wanted to know had the same kee-at got my tongue and all I said was Lookit, you sent for me, I have my bag packed for Australia and all, I have things for doing now if you don't mind. Woo-ee, says she, letting on to be all wide-eyed with surprise. Well, I'll give you till the end of today to think on, and if you change your mind, come in to me in the morning. Think on, says she, like that. Quare nordie way of talking.

I thought on anyway all that day and landed myself in at cockcrow the next day. And wasn't the whole place locked up tight and no car or anything to be seen. But when I tried the side house door wasn't it open and I pushed it before me and stood up looking in, half afraid. Out of the dark inside she arrived in her nightgown and it ending in a bit of a frill half the way down to her knee and she pulling the two sides of it tight around herself and I saw once the morning light had a chance to touch her that one side of her top lip was bloody and swollen, and there was white lines down along her face where tears had cut their marks into her. Her nose was red from snotting. There was a woeful smell of liquor about the place. Aye, says she, aye go on, fill your eyes and run away home to your mammy and daddy and tell them the blow-in got her comeuppance at last and with them words she left a pitiful cry out of her, like a keening moan really, and I'll say now in all truth I had a half a horn on me just looking at her there in her silky frilly nightgown and her bare legs and her big chest heaving and even the glisten on her face of tears and snots didn't put me off and I stepped in over the threshold and Lord strike me down now if I tell you a word of a lie but didn't I put my hand out to her in comfort and she took it in hers and without even looking up at me she put it to her breast and sure wasn't that a finish to me there and then and she knew what was after happening and she softly laughed. Go on, says she, in a whisper, hoarse and throaty kind of, and she holding out a set of keys. Open up. And off I toddled not even feeling my own discomfort and not a word came between us all that day again so shocked was I and so distracted was she by her own troubles.

She put me on a day rate after that. I was gave a station in all elements of her business. Bar, shop, yard, solid fuel. Some days was long and more was short, but the same rate paid for all. And I'd say if all was wrote down in a sum of division or done on a calculator, the money paid over the hours worked, I'd say I was always a fair whack better off than the little part-timers that came and went like the rain with their hands forever out and their fighting over shifts and rosters and days of holidays and what have you and more time gave always to arguing about work than to working.

The husband was never again seen. Maybe he telephoned or wrote to her over the years to see to know how was she getting on but as far as I know he never landed back in person. Whatever they fell out over it was a big falling-out. That it ended in his raising his hand to her was known only to me. She stayed in the back till the swelling went down and left me out to deal with people. They'd rather see your face than mine anyway, says she. You're one of them. You don't frighten them the way I do, says she. And I only barely able that time to manage the pulling of pints and the working of the till and the ham-slicer in the shop and it was all go go go for a good long while and people used be craning their necks to get a look in through the kitchen door to see where was she and what in the hell the story was and where was Himself and why in the name of Jaysus was the lad of the Farrells keeping shop here from one end of the day to the other. And I spilling whiskey into glasses like it was water, unused as I was to them auld optics and the way you must lay off the push as the bubble gets bigger and for a small while that bar once more was true to its name of The House of the Big Small Ones. And several times I wounded myself on that auld ham-slicer cleaning it and smeared the blade of it with the blood of my body. And always those evenings once all was locked up and put away and tightened up she'd put a bit of a plaster on my cut and rub my hand and stand blue-eyed barefoot before me in that short nightgown and what blood was left in me would rush to gather in the one place and my head would spin and she'd lead me by the bandaged hand to her room below down the long hall and we'd go at each other like two starved wolves going at a fat sheep.

She never asked me to know what I thought of the closing of The House of the Big Small Ones and the knocking of it and of the house attached where I had stored such fond memories and of the building of the bungalow and the big new shop like a refrigerated warehouse lit bright like a Christmas tree and it being made into first a Londis and then a Mace and of the taking on of all the little young wans and she only ever asked me to know did I know their fathers and were they any bit respectable. And she never told where was she going the times she went off in Paddy Screwballs's hackney all done up to the nines and Paddy's auld beady eye all up and down her while he lifted her leather suitcase into his boot the very same as a real how-do-you-do gentleman and I wouldn't ever give Paddy the satisfaction of asking him to know where did he drop her off but I suspect it was to the train station inside in the city for to travel north to attend family dos, weddings and what have you. And she never once asked me to know how was I after my mother passed away but I will say one thing, she gave a fair old squeeze of me at her funeral and whispered into my ear I'm sorry, I'm so so sorry, and I often wonder still was it for more than my loss of my mother she was sorry.

And over all the days and months and years we kept our goings and comings at a fair steady old rhythm.

And that hunger that came on us at times we sated with the flesh of one another.

And even when that wore off of us there was always the nearness and the certainty of one another.

And as sure as God and as sure as I'm sitting here I gave my life to her and never taught myself a thing outside or above what was needed to keep her business going and her books balanced for fear at all she'd someday up sticks and leave me.

And even my own father when he was old and faced with his end said Gor, you know, I wonder would it have been as well had I left you off that time to work with my cousin in the demolition beyond abroad the way you'd have seen something or done something, maybe.

And I took his hand and squeezed it the way I never once had when he was in his health and said No, Daddy, I was as happy here.

But happy I'll never again be, I'd say. She's gone from me now and for a finish and for good and for glory and I won't see her again. And the shop and the petrol pumps and the bungalow and the bit of money that was put away all along the years is belonging now to some nephew or other from above in the north that never in all his days set foot in this village and he wants to know will I stay on the way I can keep a good eye on things for him and I think I won't, I won't I'd say. I'll finish up this pint and go home and take off this tie that has me choked all day and tomorrow or the day after maybe I'll walk up to the Height where she asked to be buried, God alone knows why because there's no one here only me that'll ever lay a flower on her grave or pull a weed from it.

And I'll stand and say a prayer and before I turn from her I'll say Sorry, Busty, for the time I told you to go way and fuck yourself, the way I should have that time years ago when I stood unrepentant before her in her dark kitchen.

Ragnarok

THE UNIVERSE WAS once a dot, laden with the weight of everything that ever would be.

A man in a nylon shirt and unforgivable shoes came here a few days ago. You can't have four hundred students, he said. In a school with two classrooms? I uttered phrases and words strung with mumbles: short semesters, intensive modules, research courses, distance learning, assignments, assessments, awards. And on and on I went, punctuating my litany with hard sucks on my inhaler, coughs and wheezes and dissembling and obfuscation. I was fabulous. He poked his narrow nose into each room of this place. Suramon sat dutifully at his teacher's desk, facing the ranks of his invisible class. Where are your students? the poorly heeled fellow asked him. They are not here, Suramon replied, gesturing grandly at emptiness before clasping his hands tightly together on his desk. Where are they? the fellow asked again. A pen had leaked in his shirt pocket. I do not know, Suramon replied, his brown eyes twinkling as they lighted on the inky haemorrhage. Perhaps you have frightened them away.

He insisted I desisted. All scholarly activity was to cease. Pending the outcome of an investigation. I hadn't realized, I told him, that an investigation had commenced. The students were put on notice. I had a letter issued immediately to each and every one of them, to the addresses they had supplied to us at enrolment. Agata huffed and whined and pursed her heartbreaking lips. There was shuffling and banging and shouting from downstairs yesterday, raised voices, screams even. I plugged my headphones into my record player, and reclined, and listened to Olaf Aaberg singing about Ragnarok, the twilight of the gods. Olaf the Giant. Beautiful Olaf. He choked on a fishbone in a restaurant in Oslo. Ten stout men bore his pall to the flames.

A long man shouting short sentences burst in here this morning. He had men to pay. Kids to feed. He wanted what was owed to him. I felt sad for him. I told him I knew how he felt. I tried to placate him but he wouldn't stop shouting so I put my hands over my ears and closed my eyes and alternated a low hum with a loud lalalalalalala. When I opened my eyes again he was sitting silent and wide-eyed, unblinking and red. He was a rugby player once, I'm fairly sure. Thickly handsome. A backward forward. Jesus, he said, and shook his head, and hulked away. He left some papers on my desk. I haven't touched them yet. I admonished Agata for letting him in. Sorry, she said. She's very beautiful and so I forgave her. I forgive you, I told her. Oh, okay, she said, and rolled her ice-blue eyes away from me, towards heaven, and back to her magazine.

Some manner of navvy rolled in an hour or so ago. I spotted him as he skidded to a stop, lengthways across two wheelchair spaces. DENIS O'SULLIVAN BUILDING CONTRACTOR it said on the side of his van. I rang down to Agata and said under no circumstances was she to buzz him in. I am not a stupid, she said. I watched through my privacy glass as he stood roaring at the door, stabbing the buzzer. Eventually he seemed to tire and crumple; his chin dropped chestward and he was silent and still except for a slow, rhythmic shaking of his head and a corresponding hunching and dropping of his broad shoulders. He pulled the windscreen wipers from a Mercedes that he must have supposed was mine before he left. I don't know whose it really is. One of those chaps from the auditors next door, I suppose. A pair of bored and oily men came to the house for my car weeks ago. They attached a hook and chain to it and dragged it onto their truck-bed. Olive cried and hid from the neighbours. I've been driving her Micra since. It's a slow and uncomplicated little thing. Just like Olive.

Another breaking voice on the phone. Something about the apartments we were building. Who's we? Me and my echo. Me and my impatient ghost. I am a director of seven companies. I can't remember all their names. Workers protesting, occupying the sites. Union goons on colliding warpaths. Subcontractors suing. All the pies my fingers were in are stale and crumbling. But still my fingers won't come out. Something else about the horse. Lame, or dead. Olive's voice on the phone, tear-strangled and shrill. Something else about our daughter, or our son, or a credit limit reached, or breached, or rescinded. Agata swept in and brought clarity with her. She hasn't smiled at me in weeks. There's a light I can move towards: a smile from her. I took four folded fifties from my wallet for her weekly 'expenses' and watched her perfect closed face as I handed them to her and she glanced at them and secreted them fluidly in some dark delicious fold. I ache to follow the money in there, to hide in the hills and valleys of her. Busy, busy, she said. Yes, I agreed, happily abetting her lie. She pierced me with a sigh and left, taking a random folder with her.

Pyrite, someone was saying just then. I'm not sure exactly when. Blocks crumbling like Weetabix. Class action. There was something on the radio about this the other day but Olive's stereo emits mostly static since she left her aerial up in the carwash. Thank God, I thought, we escaped that one, at least. Now here it is, joining with the others at the mouth of my cave. A pack of red-eyed fang-bared beasts, sensing my weakening, slavering, waiting for my fire to die so that they can enter and devour me flesh and bone. Agata will tend the flames and hold them at bay. Until the firing runs out. I haven't many fifties left.

A cave with Agata. Me in a bearskin, she in her bare skin. My head spins as my blood is summoned to its most base and necessary duty. I should eat. Olive hands me something in the mornings as I leave, pungent and seed-covered, casketed in Tupperware. I thank her and I kiss her cold cheek and I empty the box into the dog before I drive away. If Olive died this day I'd cash her in and run. I'd stop in Paris on the way east and show Agata the Place de la Concorde. I'd kiss her by that phallic rune that was heaved there from some eastern place; I'd ask her to say that she loved me. That lie from her lips would be sweeter than any everyday truth.

My man in Bangladesh is still recruiting happily. If he gets me twenty more that's sixty grand, enough to float my canoe downriver from this creek. We know all about your agent, the plastic-shoed fellow from earlier in the week said. Your agent is a visa salesman, he said. That's defamatory, I replied. Oh, he said, is it? I thought defamation required an absence of truth? And he slammed an A4 page of foreign words on my desk and he raised his grisly mono-brow and smiled. I've never seen that before, I told him, and he told me that I was not obliged to say anything and so I said nothing except Get new fucking shoes. His biro had pissed itself all over his shirt by then and he still hadn't noticed. But the shoes were the worst of all.

A noise from across the room, near the filing cabinet. Agata let the cleaner in, then. How long ago, I wonder. A different one comes each time. Twice a week, I'm nearly sure. A man with a ratty face and hooded eyes undercut the last crowd by fifteen per cent. How is that possible? I asked him. Oh, he said, there's loads of ways, all legal and all, like, of getting round all a them things that makes business impossible to do. His breath stank of dead things. Sure you know yourself, he said. I do, I do, I agreed pleasantly from behind my left hand, which was clamped across my nose and mouth. He didn't seem to notice; he only had eyes for my right hand, which was signing his little contract.

The cleaner has an Aztec cast to her features. She's young, brimming, strong-legged and squat. Shapely rump, though, and a tight black skirt. Has she an indolent husband, I wonder, in a pitiless *favela*, chewing the shoots of some opiate plant in a shanty's lee, awaiting her airmailed wages? So he can swagger and swan and squander the price of her labour in some flyblown hooch-dive. Has she babies left behind, in the care of other mothers? The ache in her, the sorrow in her brown eyes. She has an extraordinary chest. Up the walls, she says, looking nervously at me, smiling into silence, as she upends my wastepaper basket into her refuse bag. A sweet and guileless affectation, projecting the vernacular of here onto that of there, a spoken palimpsest.

Olive will die soon enough. All of her womenfolk were smote early, her mother and aunts and sisters, by diseases that seem to prey on slight and nervous women. They all succumbed quietly, obligingly, and left their men to their horses and golf and secretaries. I'll miss her shuffling presence when she's gone. My chiselling indifference eroded her. I never loved her enough. I don't know if I loved her at all, or how I'd know, at this remove. I can't remember how I was then, when I was young. I could have another life as long again as this one's been. I'll have to become something to which squalor is suited. A writer, maybe, or a painter, sleeping on an ancient ornate bed in the corner of a wide and open garret, dissected in the day by sunbeams in which fiery dust-motes dance. Jars upon jars of brushes in water, tubes and charcoal and bottles and palettes and canvases covered in dashes and daubs to which others can ascribe meaning. Or reams of paper covered in jostling words, mugs of pens and chewed pencils, an ancient Underwood set before a sunlit wall on a table of oak, chipped and stained.

I gave a man with dark blue eyes a cheque one day for a share in a seven-star hotel on a heart-shaped island in a shimmering silvery inland sea. He smiled at me and shook my hand and his footsteps rang loud on the floor as he left. Cloven feet, I thought, and laughed to myself, and laughed and laughed. Agata drank champagne with me that afternoon and early evening and sat for a while on my lap. I went home in a taxi, with a light head and leaden balls. The island sank and all the things upon it were drowned and the souls who could not strike for shore were lost. I never again saw that blue-eyed man but I felt his presence once or twice behind me, and turned and there was no one there.

My father was always happy to see me. Ah, there you are, he'd say, and smile, as if we had been in one another's company all along, filling time in some gentle, pleasant way, and had been momentarily separated. He had a weakness one day and he fell on the street and was taken by force to a hospital where he was poked and scanned and told he was dying. Too much of the good life, he said. Isn't it grand all the same, he said, to be dying from a good life, and not from a bad life? Aren't I as lucky as bedamned? And he drove to Coonagh Cross and checked and filled and primed his Cessna and arced that sparrow heavenward and pulled back hard on the throttle and jammed it open. He'd have laughed into the blue and passed into blackness before the rivets gave. I wouldn't have the guts for that. But nor have I the guts for this.

How long has Agata been standing at the open office door, I wonder, with that look of disgust on her face? How long have my tears been turning my visitors' documents to pulp? How long has the cleaner been standing beside my chair, shushing me softly, her warm hand on mine?

And to a dot it will return, laden with the weight of everything that ever was.

Physiotherapy

I SQUEEZE THE rubber ball three times and raise my arm so that my left hand meets his right and he always seems to smile as he takes the ball from me and grips it softly and I nod three times at him in time with his three squeezes. He reaches across himself with his good left arm and takes the ball from himself and repeats the exercise and I take it in my right and so on and so on and so on. The physiotherapist gave us a long-handled stick with a netted scoop at its end to retrieve the ball when we drop it the way we wouldn't be hauling ourselves up and out of our chairs and exhausting ourselves before we have our exercises done. Why don't you just give us a square ball the way it won't roll, I said to him, and he got a bit sour I think, and muttered something about the bones of our hands or some such. He reminded me of a nephew of mine I haven't seen for a long time. A curly-headed lad, long in the back and longer in the face, my sister Noreen's boy, gone off to London or somewhere but years and years. A lot of them get lost out foreign, they don't come back themselves.

We were married at twenty, Pierse and me. He was older by a week exactly. I wore a simple white dress my mother made for me, and he wore a navy suit borrowed from his father's brother who was about his size. We had our wedding breakfast inside in O'Meara's Hotel and only our families were there and my friend Theresa who was maid-of-honour and his friend Mossy who was best man. We went for a week to Galway on our honeymoon in a Volkswagen Beetle lent to us by the manager of the co-op, who was a friend of Pierse's father. Pierse held my hand every minute of every day, hardly letting me go even while we ate. I sat on his lap in our narrow suite and he hugged me fiercely, and he kissed my mouth and face and eyes. We adventured up and down narrow streets and watched fishermen on the quays as they inspected their nets in the mornings and hauled their catches in the evenings and Pierse tried a few words of Irish out on a chap one day and the chap only smiled and didn't answer and Pierse smiled into the quayside stench and reddened so deeply I thought he'd burst.

Pierse got into auctioneering through another friend of his father's and he quickly gained a reputation for thoroughness and honesty and there was never a trace of sneakiness that was ever known about him, and people could see that in the first few instants of knowing him. He grew inches at an auction; it was the only place that time he seemed to fit, it was as though his gavel protected him from embarrassment, as though his practised ululations, inscrutable to me, threw up a wall of strength around him. Men as seemingly straight and quiet in their ways as him stood watching, nodding their bids, hardly seeming to care about the outcome. Pierse spoke slowly and clearly to potential buyers of houses, pointing out where work needed to be done, where things could be improved. He couldn't do the hard sell, he couldn't stretch the truth. Eventually there was a falling-out and he came home one evening and sat after dinner for longer than he usually did and our son looked with concern at him as he excused himself and went looking for his hurley and ball and he told me after long minutes that he wouldn't be going back to Woodley and Woodley as there were underhand dealings going on and he couldn't be a part of them. He started to buy old rundown houses and renovate them and sell them for an honest profit and he made good money and seemed happy with his work, but it never made him as tall as he used to seem at his lectern, sweeping his gaze, am-bidding, gavel in hand.

I wonder what he thinks about all the day long. I should know, I suppose, or would, if I was any kind of a wife. Silence always suited him. That his silence now has been forced upon him by sickness hardly matters. I think a lot about the day he stole into the house through the back porch door and a present in his hand for me of a gold necklace with a heart on it and a diamond set in its centre and I sitting in the dining room at the table with James and his hand on mine and he gripping my fingers so tightly his knuckles were white. And a fool could know what was happening, what had happened, what had been about to happen. And he only punished me for that with silence. He left himself out through the front door and went down the avenue to his car that he had parked down there away from the house the way I wouldn't hear him coming in and he could surprise me, back early from his trip to the north, and the necklace boxed and bowed and held out before him like a thing being taken altarward in an offertory procession and the thorns of the rosebush opened the skin of my hand as I retrieved it from where he'd flung it and the salt of my tears seared in the tiny wounds.

I finished it with James that day and never took up with another man again. Pierse ended his self-imposed exile from our bed after a few weeks but he got into the habit of staying up watching television at night, and drinking, never very much, but enough so that he'd sleep sedated and the smell of it would drift from his breath across to me. He was never bothered by the silence between us, only the loudness, when I'd burst out with something, to try to goad him, to wound him, to make him react in some way so that I could say There's the long and the short of it, there's what he feels; now I can know what I need to do to repay. But all debts are written off eventually, when it's clear no payment will ever be made, that restitution isn't possible and everything is then reset to nought.

Pierse took to holding my hand daily again after our son died. As though to stop the shaking in himself, he gripped me, and took both my hands in his, and squeezed his eyes closed and bared his teeth and his breaths would rush and heave from him like silent screams. He'd helped him buy his ticket to Australia; he'd even contacted some people he knew over there to arrange a few weeks or maybe months of work for him on building sites, and he'd driven him to the airport and hugged him awkwardly but tightly at the departure gate and showed no sign of letting go until Stephen pulled back gently laughing from him. He asked me did I want to stop somewhere for a bit to eat on the way home and I said yes and we stopped in Limerick and in a corner table of a darkened restaurant he'd sat in front of a plate of untouched food and said Christ, Maud, I think I'm after making an awful mistake. Letting him off like that. I should have persuaded him to stay here and work away with me. And not three weeks later our telephone rang in the early hours and he took my hand as we walked up the hall from our bedroom and a voice half a world away told us our Stephen was gone, scaffolding had collapsed under him and he had been killed.

There are days when it seems as though they are the only three things to ever have happened. I got married, I had a love affair, my son was killed. Someone now, some expert in the ways of human minds, looking from a cold distance at me and at the way I carried on, would say I was suffering then from some kind of depression or disorder or some such nonsense. But James stole into my life smiling, and the sight of him, his presence in a room, caused the air to thicken, my mind to slow, my heart to quicken. I don't understand fully still to this day what came over me, or out of me, or what kind of a spell he cast on me, but I nearly drowned myself in foolishness and heat. The noise of those days, the burning joy, the wildness. He was a young widower; his wife had haemorrhaged in childbirth, his daughter was born to sadness and he told me these things in a soft voice, and he told me how he loved to talk to me, how he loved to look at my eyes, how he loved me. He kissed me and I lost my reason. When the church roof was mended and the fundraising committee we co-chaired was disbanded he came to our house and sat in the dining room and gripped this hand so hard it pained me and he asked me to come away with him and his teenaged daughter to England, and to bring little Stephen with me, and I nearly said yes until some gentle draught Pierse created in his effort to surprise me caused me to turn my head and see him there, at that doorway, with his gift for me on the palm of his trembling hand.

We're going well now, with our ball. The squeezing and passing from left hand to right hand to partner, and the wait to take it back, have fallen to an easy rhythm. Our knees are almost touching, I can feel the warmth of him. A strange, fortunate symmetry, that his left side was struck and my right, his within six months of mine. Mini-strokes, the doctors said. There'll be more, as likely as not. Tremors before the earthquakes. The ball falls from his hand; he sucks his teeth in crossness at himself. He looks at me, he stretches out his arm. He grips my hand and pulls lightly and I use the last of my fleeing strength to cross the space between us and turn myself so that I'm sitting on his lap. My necklace swings outwards, the little heart describes an arc and settles again on my chest. I'm seventy-seven and I'm twenty, my child is dead and he hasn't yet been born, there's a thickening of the air about me again in this day room, in this honeymoon suite, and my heart is slowing and my mind is quickening and the arms are tight around me and the breath and tears are on my face of the man I pledged to God to love and honour all my days.

Long Puck

MY FIRST WEDNESDAY here the Orthodox Christian priest strode in long-bearded and black-eyed. He embraced me and kissed me on my cheeks, he in a frock and me in a smock, and he called me Brother. Being green and unsure of the prevailing custom I only stood and smiled at him and he smiled back at me with his hands on my shoulders and said, We will be friends. And he strode back out and across and up the wide and dusty street to his own tiny stone church. It's peaceful here, my oldest parishioner told me. There was a thing once, a terrible thing that happened, but it was a hotness of the blood, a sudden, silly thing, young men . . . And he trailed off and said no more about it and I thought no further about his intimations and worked each day in the cool inside of my church and welcomed all who entered here.

A local boy in his late teens or early twenties came here one day and said his name was Halim and asked did I know a place called Tipperary. It's where I'm from, I told him. He laughed and a light in his eyes danced. His cousin lived there. What is this place like? he asked. I told him about the green fields and low hills and forests and valleys and the villages and towns and the speedy drawly talk of the people. They must like chips, he said. My cousin is a rich man. He drives a Mercedes. He sells chips at curling matches in the summer. Hurling, I corrected him. I showed my new friend my hurley and sliotar, and pucked it against the transept wall. His eyes widened. I rang home for another hurley. It came with a shipment of vestments and wine. He'd come to the church in the cooling evening and say, Few pucks, Father? And every time I heard these words I laughed and he laughed with me and we pucked our sliotar up and down the street.

It became a thing in the town, a break in the sunwashed greyness. The hurleys and the sliotar and the priest. Slitter, shlitter, pucks, hoorleys, hurlings, roars of laughter. An imam strolled slowly down to our quarter one still day and watched silently, then smiled at me and asked could he try. He threw the sliotar and swung wildly and missed and my young friend Halim laughed and quickly caught himself. He spoke gently with careful deference to the old man and I saw by his gestures he was telling him to throw the ball slightly higher and farther outwards from his body, to keep his eye on it all the time, to grip with his left hand lower. The imam connected cleanly on his third try and smiled in satisfaction. He raised his hand and bowed slightly and walked back towards his mosque.

A band of hooting watchers formed. We took to having our few pucks at the same time each evening, after their prayers and our devotions. The hurleys were passed from hand to hand; some quickly caught the hang of it, more swung wild and awkward and rarely connected. When leather fell square and clean on ash and my sliotar soared skyward a roar went up and rose with the swirling dust raised by the minor stampede of men and boys trying to catch the falling ball. A man brought a baseball catcher's mitt one day and the others booed. He handed it shamefaced to me and pretended he had brought it as a gift.

I rang home for as many hurleys as could be sent. A note came one day from the station that there was a delivery waiting there for me. My curate, a small and quiet man from Clare, handed it to me with a ghost of a smile; we walked through the market and past the commercial quarter and the old traders' mansions and along the open railway that flanked the olive plantation to the paved widening in the street of dust and stones that served as the train station. We hefted a dozen hurleys home. My quiet curate sweated under his burden of ash. He tutted and huffed and muttered under his breath about me and my blasted hurleys. But when we grounded our load in the sacristy he exhaled loudly and I saw on his face a smile of tired satisfaction, and I heard him later as I stood unseen by him at the altar door, blessing the heap of hurleys and all who would play with them.

The first long puck competition was held the same day the idea of it was conceived. Landed balls were marked in dust and each man stood by his line. Arguments over whose was which threatened to end badly, until the Orthodox lad offered to officiate. A hundred yards was measured with a hand-rolled odometer borrowed from the municipal authority by the cousin of a friend of a hurler called Ahmed. Pucks were measured back from or up from the hundred-yard line. Ah lads, call a howlt, I'd shout in an exaggerated Irish accent if a row broke out, and they'd echo me, laughing. Ah lads, call a howlt! would ring along the sun-baked street as far as the marketplace. I got off a good one, clean and high. At least fifteen yards out from the previous leader. Applause rippled upwards from the marketplace like a handful of pebbles landing in water. Halim stepped up next and smiled at me before launching a sliotar skyward. It will come down with snow on it, eh, Father? And we laughed as the Orthodox priest shouted, Tie! It is a dead tie!, and supporters of my friend Halim protested and measured with fingers and feet and squinted eyes and declared Halim the champion and the competition to be a fix. The decision that one last puck each would decide the day was greeted with silence, then Ha-*lim*, Ha-*lim*, chanted rhythmically, rising in speed and volume as my friend toed the line we had drawn in the dust and swung in a tidy and powerful arc and sent the ball buzzing low and fast through the still and heavy air. I shook Halim's hand before taking my shot and he smiled at me nodding and my curate suddenly broke free of his quietness and roared Go on, Father Anthony, give it holly, lash into it! But my ball fell short of the mark that was scraped in the dust of the street moments earlier and Halim was hoisted shoulder-high and carried off a hero.

Tell me words said in Tipperary, Halim would say. Words of the people who would buy chips from my cousin.

Well, youssir, how you keeping?

Yerra shur I'm only dragging.

Soft day, thank God.

Begod tis.

Garlic chip and cheese, two battered sausage there please, I'd ate shtones I'm so hungry.

No bother, boy, gimme wan minute.

And on and on I'd go, filling Halim's head with paddywhackery. He'd ring his cousin before our pucks the odd evening from a brick of a mobile. Hey, you sir, you're some stones, this is Paddy here, from over beyond, will you do me up a takeaway until I collect it? I'd ate the arse of a low-flying duck, so I would. I'll have . . . And he'd laugh and laugh until he could hardly breathe and his cousin's roars of laughter in faraway Tipp would crackle through the ancient Nokia and Halim would declare that one day he'd see this place, Tipperary, and hear these words spoken in truth, and see these mighty hurling men. He would shake Brendan Cummins by the hand, the man with the longest puck in all of Tipperary. All of Ireland? Yes. The world? Maybe, probably.

My bishop arrived from the capital in a stately old Mercedes driven by a man who hunched himself in a semi-circle over the steering wheel. He was weary, languorous, unsmiling. We concelebrated and had dinner and the town's prominent Catholics were invited and he was gifted specially imported cognac and local wine and olive oil. As his crescent-shaped man waited at the wheel of his idling car to return him to his palace the next day he proffered his ring dourly and said, Enough with the games. And then he was gone.

I wrote a letter to Jimmy Ryan in Newport asking for a hurley for a lad of five feet eleven, with a good bas, not quite goalkeeper size, and a grand light handle. I asked would he put a grip on it in the blue and gold of Tipperary and send it in as far as Nenagh to Brother John Daly who I wanted to write a message along the length of it in calligraphy with an indelible marker. I felt a prickle of excitement each time I thought of myself presenting Halim with his gift, crafted by Jimmy Ryan of Newport, a legendary maker of hurleys.

Clouds rolled in around that time, at the start of winter. Flurries of violence in the distant capital, lightning protests quickly doused. Militias formed in the provinces, government troops massed at flashpoints and hotspots and strongholds. Halim's hurley arrived in the town on the same train that brought two dozen dark-eyed, laughless men with guns of unreflecting metal. The Muslim women veiled more fully and walked and dressed with greater observance than before, never venturing past their doorsteps without a male relative a step or two in front of them. The Orthodox Christians and the Catholics for the most part stayed at home, behind their gates. The olive plantation slowed production; three of their trucks were requisitioned. The police were nowhere to be seen. I had never hefted a hurley so perfect.

Halim stood across the street from my church, facing east, not facing in. He was shifting his weight from foot to foot, stroking his new beard furiously, darting looks around in all directions except mine. I walked across to him. I didn't bring my gift for him from its resting place beside the holy-water font. He stood at a right angle from me as he spoke. All sorts of accusations had been levelled against him by his mother's cousin. Apostasy had been whispered. He had been questioned by a group of the newcomers. Why was he friends with a Catholic priest? What were these games he played? Who else was involved in this group that hit balls with sticks up and down the streets? They were rebels, and were gathering all the men to fight. Sharia was to be observed in its fullness, apostates were to be killed, infidels driven out. Leave, my friend, Halim said. Today. And the sun flashed a spear of light from the tear at the side of his eye. As he walked away I saw that he was limping heavily, his left hand pressed against his ribs.

Scattered showers of shells fell on the outskirts of the town but government forces largely bypassed us at the start. My curate said We really ought to leave. I told him go if he wanted. I declared my church a refuge for all. Mass would be said daily and devotions would be at the usual time each evening. I hurled my sliotar up against the transept wall for thirty minutes after devotions without fail. Government forces woke fully to our town, realized we had become a stronghold, a hotbed, an enclave. Short warning was given, a helicopter gunship on a reconnaissance flight above us was shot at by hotheads and that was all that was needed. The gunship retraced its earlier route, lower, its nose angled more steeply down as though the machine itself was peering, searching. Again the rebels fired on it and on its third looping sortie it was spitting death. The olive plantation lorries that had returned two days previously were rolled to the town square and ancient-looking mortar cannons were taken from beneath the tarpaulin on their flatbeds and embedded in the hard ground. Three-man mortar teams were assembled. Co-ordinates were hastily applied, and the rebels began a vaguely aimed pounding of guessed-at government positions.

My curate begged me to stay inside, to join him as he sat worrying his rosary beads against the stoutest column in the nave, beneath the sturdiest centre arch. Let them come, I roared, and swung my hurley as fiercely as my muscles would allow, and sweated in the still dry heat. People carried children and belongings through my church's door and camped beneath sheets between pews shoved back to back. I asked nothing of anyone. Government troops laid light siege at first, tightening inwards slowly with the days. The rebels held the centre.

They came in ragged battle dress through our gate three days ago, six of them, in two rows. Halim was left half-forward. There were Christians and Muslims and agnostics at shelter from the storm of fire in the coolness of the inside of my church. The big lad at full-forward swung his arm back and caught Halim by the front of his jersey and dragged him forward and out to the front. Halim looked at the ground before him and up at me and around at his cowering homeless neighbours and he pointed up at Our Lord, a long finger unfurled from a shaking hand. His other hand gripped the wooden stock of an automatic rifle. Leave this place, he roared, and the suddenness and the pitch of it startled me. I wasn't sure in my shock was he addressing Christ or me. Leave this place, *FATHER*, and he didn't look at me but he spat the word. His comrades stood behind and before me; I was shoved in the back and shoved from the front until my knees weakened and I was suddenly kneeling. A rifle-butt struck the floor before me. Your saviour-on-a-stick won't help you if you're still here tomorrow, a voice not Halim's said. And Our Lord on His Cross was taken from above my altar and smashed and splintered across the flagstones. As they left I saw Halim stop beside the holy-water font. I saw him see his gift and the words along it and he looked back at me and his face had a shadow across it not made by the sun. And then he was gone.

They came again the next day, and this time there were no words spoken to me. Four of them had their rifles slung across their backs while two of them flanked and pointed, swinging their barrels around in slow, threatening arcs. I recognized one of them as one of our earliest hurlers, a friend of Halim's, a happy, smiling fellow who had always worn an Arsenal jersey and asked me once could I tell him the best way to become a doctor. How swiftly men are robbed of light. The four scanned the refugees on the floor of my church and grabbed a man each and dragged their prisoners crying away. I stood in the doorway, my brave curate to my right, and he was shot in the chest and the round made a hole in him through which I could briefly see the sixth station of the cross on the far wall and the word KINDNESS carved below it and the butt of a rifle sent stars and sky reeling down around my head.

I rose from the floor a short while ago and saw my church was empty of living people, abandoned belongings scattered and streeled. I walked slowly across the courtyard to the gate and looked through my half-open eyes along the street. The Orthodox priest who kissed me and embraced me one time not so long ago and called me Brother and umpired a long puck competition or two is sprawled on the path before his church, a billow of black smoke behind him, a halo of blood around his head, dancing flames reflected in his open unseeing eyes. Icons have been arranged around him in a circle and set alight, accidentally almost heart-shaped. Accidentally I think, anyway. It's hard to know now. Probably it always was. I just never knew before how hard it is to really and truly know anything.

I'm settled now in the nave, in the seat left empty by my curate who lies still where he fell, and I see through the porch and the open door that they're back, and all I have as weapon against them is this hurley, with the words *Halim Assam, All-Syria Long Puck Champion 2012* inscribed along the perfect shaft of it in beautiful calligraphy.

Losers Weepers

THE WORLD IS FILLED with unwelcome words. Insolvent. Bankrupt. Unfriended. Someone did that to my daughter yesterday, and she's been pale and silent ever since. All I could do was say Don't worry, love, my love, don't cry. He couldn't have been your real friend to start with. And she sobbed and nodded and tried to hide her pain behind her laptop screen.

There's a shadow moving slowly outside in the orange arc-sodium light. Up and down the cul-de-sac. A neighbour who's lost her engagement ring. It's worth seven grand. I know because she told me in a desperate whisper as I helped her search for it earlier. Oh, God, I know, it's only a ring, she kept saying, it's only a *ring*. Her husband's working in Canada.

Unfriended. It's not even a proper verb, only an ugly confection of a word to describe the deletion of a thing that never really existed. Amber looked at me as she told me about it through eyes ringed with livid red and she was a child again. I wanted to run to the place where the unfriender lived and kick down his door and choke the life from his miserable teenaged body. But all I could do was say Don't worry, love, please don't cry.

My neighbour couldn't say the words for a while. She was careful with them. She didn't want to cry in front of me, this stranger she'd been living not thirty yards from for at least four years. My . . . engagement . . . ring. I'd been meaning to get it reduced. I was walking, just up and down the cul-de-sac, with the buggy. Trying to get my little man off to sleep. He's a pure little crank, so he is. It must have just . . . slipped off. I'd never have left the house without it. And she placed a long and delicate-looking hand across her mouth and squeezed her eyes closed for a second or two, a flimsy barricade hastily thrown up against a procession of tears. How can I not find it? How can it not be here? How did I not feel it slipping off? And she looked accusingly at another unaware neighbour, driving slowly towards home. I never saw so many *fucking cars* around here, she said, and looked suddenly shocked at herself. Oh, no, I just meant . . . you know. I know, I said, and smiled at her and looked quickly back at the ground.

The day I opened my shop nine years ago I overheard my mother talking to my aunt. How is it at all none of mine could be any way cute? They haven't a dust between them, God help us. A *camera* shop, I *ask* you. The barest breeze of hardship will blow it away. And Aunty Susan sighed and shook her head and dragged deeply on her fag in sympathy and sorrow.

We trawled the footpaths and the tarmacadam with our eyes. We sifted through patches of gravel and pebbles with our fingers. We braved the sting of kerbside thistles. We were forensic about it. We're like the crowd in *CSI Miami*, someone joked, an older man whose face we all knew well but whose name was known to none. Paddy. He was surprised we didn't know his name. Sure we're here years and years, Mary and me. Oh God, ya. There was only our house here starting off. Sure this was the countryside not so long ago. All ye crowd are only Johnny-come-latelies. And he beamed around at everyone, happy to be the one doing all the talking, and we smiled embarrassedly back. We should all have known him well.

Mother drained her champagne flute on my opening day and held it before her, squinting at it with a grimace. Lord Almighty that's as sour as gall. Oul cheap stuff, that is. Susan rounded a bit then, as Mother's eyeballs swivelled heavenward in disgust.

They say the best stuff is always the bitterest, Elsie. Mother's eyes narrowed again, her nostrils flared. Well, go get two more then if you're such an expert till I anaesthetize myself. And I stepped unseen backwards, away from her, and sat for a while in the cool silence of my shining new staff bathroom with that old familiar stinging at the backs of my eyes.

By three o'clock there were nine searchers. A sudden solidarity blossomed in the neighbourhood. Friendly enquiries as to what's been lost led to sympathetic small-talk, offers of assistance and tea, anecdotes of ancient losses and miraculous finds: watches, wallets, lockets, twenty-pound notes; lifetimes of misplaced things that all made their ways back. No one dwelt too much on the things they never saw again or the dark, iron-grilled storm-drains that line our road or the magpies that patrol the hedges and the carpets of grass.

Lord, wasn't it a great idea? My father kind of claimed it as his own. We couldn't keep the shop stocked. He'd call in at least once most weeks and smile at my customers. He searched, often vainly, for common ground. The rugby, the horses, the football. He'd wink over at me. Sure I'd sell snow to Eskimos, son. He'd stand in behind the counter and offer advice. Oh, that's a right yoke. That's a great choice. I have one of them at home myself. What about a case for it? Here, I'll throw it in. And he'd summon Mikhail to ring up the sale, tersely instructing him to apply arbitrary discounts. Mikhail would complain to me. He makes these things up half of the time, you know. He does not know the things about photography he say he knows. He gives away the profit margin with the free stuff. *Free!* Ah Dad, I'd say jokily, come out from behind the counter. You're upsetting Mikhail. Dad would harrumph and regard Mikhail darkly. Watch that fella, son, I'm telling you. Them lads are only ever out for themselves as a rule. Don't worry, Dad, I'd say. Come on and we have a small one in the snug. And Mikhail would come and they'd make it up and Dad would call him Mickey and tell him he was a grand lad and punch him lightly on the arm.

Amber joined the search. The unfriending was pushed away for a while. Who's this lovely-looking girl, now, Paddy wanted to know. I didn't know we had a . . . whatdoyoucallum . . . *supermodel* in the neighbourhood! And Amber smiled and Paddy laughed loudly and repeated his joke a few times. God aye, ya. A supermodel, begor. Paddy is kind and avuncular, the type of man who can say these things about a sixteen-year-old without sounding inappropriate. The neighbours laughed as they searched and Amber blushed and smiled and fixed her eyes to the ground.

I thought I was tough. I thought I was knock-hardened, world-wise, astute. I supplied a hotel with thirty-three grand's worth of video and hi-fi equipment. I smiled to myself as I tucked a jocular note into the envelope with the invoice. To Steve, their financial controller. Sound man, Steve. This order would be the saving of us. I went through seven or eight compliment slips in an effort to look casual. It had to be clear but slightly scrawled; professional but a bit throwaway, like I posted invoices this size every day. I was so proud of that invoice. I thought about leaving a copy of it magnetized to my fridge for the next time my parents called. I wrote something about golf and drinks and God knows what. I spent long pleasant minutes thinking how best to sign it off. Yours. Regards. Best. I settled on Thanks. Again. I considered for a minute slipping a sweetener in with it. A crisp folded fifty, for good luck. Then decided it would be crass. Best to treat him to lunch, or dinner and drinks. I thought about how I'd fill a wicker hamper as a Christmas box for my new best customers. My new friends. I thought about the power of networking.

Paddy became the foreman of the search. We're at nothing,

lads, just milling around like this. We need to divide the road into sections. Now, Deirdre love, tell us again where you definitely remember walking. Right, right, okay, look, I'll assign a section so to everyone and no one is to step outside their section till we've it found. Any cars that come to the entrance we'll tell them park up and walk. Now, there's another thing, we'll have to check the treads of the tyres of any cars that drove up since it was lost. And nearly everyone automatically obeyed, glad that someone was taking charge. A teenage boy sloped away with a regretful look back at Amber.

A month after I posted the invoice I stood smiling a little nervously at the shop door, watching the postman and his bicycle process down the street. He had nothing for me but a salute and a cool breeze as he pedalled past. I wasn't worried. No one paid exactly on time. Well, I did, but I was a bit obsessive that way. At the next month's end I sent a second invoice. Ten days. A slightly less light-hearted note. A wastepaper basket full of crumpled compliment slips. Another week passed before I heard the union rep on the radio. Staff shocked. No warning. No notice. Doors locked. Wedding deposits should be claimed in writing. The creditors' meeting was held in a GAA clubhouse on the windy end of a narrow peninsula in south Kerry. A right stroke that was. Real toughness. I got lost and missed most of it. Steve wasn't at the meeting. Distance to Empty: 23 miles, my dashboard told me as I pulled out of the potholed car-park. It was nearly sixty miles to home. I pulled into a lay-by and found seven-forty in change beneath the seats and nearly cried with relief. My hands shook as I counted it out in the petrol station.

The neighbour, Deirdre, drafted in her mother-in-law to watch her five-year-old and her six-month-old. The older woman stood at the front door for most of the evening surveying the search. Whenever I looked in her direction she smiled and nodded her thanks. Her son was half a world away and her grandson was swaddled in her arms against the chill of evening. She was weighed down with sadness and worry and love. I knelt down to peer along the ground beneath a car that had been checked a dozen times already and groaned as I straightened. She beckoned me to the doorway where she stood. You'd want to mind your back. And then she leaned forward, raising the child almost to her cheek as she did so, and whispered conspiratorially: It's gone, I'd say. Poor Deirdre, it won't be found now. Someone has it taken, surely. Ye may give it up and go in out of the cold. And you'd want to mind your back.

I stood in my father's garden a few hours ago beneath a branch heavy with pink-white blossoms. How're things, son? Grand. You're kept going? I am. Good, begod. And he smiled and sighed and put a hand to the tree's gnarled trunk to steady himself. The sky was suddenly black with crows. Dad? Are you okay? I'm fine. There they are, look. Going home. The same time every single evening. Lord save us aren't they a sight? The ring in my jeans pocket must have been sitting on an artery; I could feel my pulse beneath it.

It's only a ring. There's a stand in the shopping centre beneath a golden cardboard euro sign manned by a smiling youth with a knot in his tie like a fist. I'll go in when it's quiet, in the early morning maybe, and he'll turn the ring into a small pile of cash. That'll keep us in gas and electricity and groceries for a few months.

The shadow still moves outside. A prayer to Saint Anthony drifts through my open window on a gentle breeze. The world is filled with unwelcome words.

Grace

THERE WERE TWO boys sitting in the centre of the bus this morning. The only empty seats were across from and in front of them. Their fellow travellers in silent concord had quarantined them. The one on the outside was wan and shaven-headed. His leg was extended across the aisle, blocking it. He did not move as I approached, only held my eyes with his and smiled. His smile was twisted and wet, and brought a memory to me of the dogs that would stalk one another about the township, some days in uneasy league with one another and other days in ragged battle. His trousers had stripes that, when I looked more closely, revealed themselves to be tiny shadow-women, sitting back-to-back, in a line along the length of his leg. I smiled at the sight of them, and laughed when I saw that the ends of these trousers were tucked inside white socks. His foot was splayed outwards in a dirty training shoe. The fuck, he said, in a questioning way, half turning towards his friend, widening his eyes in mock wonderment. The *fuck*? And I knew then that these boys were going to try to hurt me in some way, that they would be allowed to do so by the others on the bus, and I wondered again how there could be pleasure in the causing of sadness in others, how a healthy young man in a country of such fertile soil could choose to expend his precious energy in such a wretched pursuit.

A woman I work with says all the time that she is afraid of her life. I laughed when I first heard this. Afraid of your life? You should be more afraid of your death, I said, and thought that she would laugh. But she didn't smile or give any sign that she had heard me as she went on moving dust from place to place with a feathery stick and explained that she was afraid of her life she'd be caught working. She is not supposed to work, as I am not. She claims to have nothing in order to claim money from the government. I claim to stay all day in the reception centre while I wait for my application for asylum to be processed, a grey building of four hollow floors, but in truth I could not stay alone there. I'd do this job for nothing, just to be away from that place, busy, moving. I'm afraid of my life, Grace; she says to me, I'm afraid of my Jaysus life. And I laugh softly to myself and tell her not to worry, not to worry, as we work on into the darkness.

The victory my father achieved in the village was of a particular type. I cannot remember at this remove the correct name for it. A priest told it to me who visited our school in the township after I had explained to the class how our family had come to leave the village of my birth. My sister scolded me for being so foolish, for being so free with truth. As though our story was some form of currency. The meaning of the word the white-haired priest put on Father's victory was that more was lost in battle than was gained in victory. I wish I could remember that word.

My father refused to pay a tribute to the elders from our harvest. Let them raise their own, he yelled, and our neighbours clicked their tongues and sighed but stayed mostly silent. No one came to help with the saving of our crop. The rains came while we laboured and washed our wealth away. My father bellowed at the gushing sky as my mother stood silent behind him, wringing her hands. The elders decreed that we were to be shunned. So tall my father was as we began our journey to Kinshasa, so noble and unswerving as he led us through the centre of the village. No man dared impede him, or mock him to his face. The elders' eyes followed him; they mourned their drowned tribute.

Shortly after I told that story in the school my father crossed me from the page in his heart that bore his children's names. My fourteenth winter was spent in the house of my mother's cousin, a shack of tin and discarded timber. My father left me there with instructions to him to see that I continued to attend the missionary school. He would pay him for my keep as soon as he found work. My mother's cousin laughed as my parents left with my brothers and sisters strung in a sullen line behind them. A holy man came once to the house and remonstrated with my mother's cousin. He was unmarried, living with a child not his. Stories were being told. People wouldn't tolerate it. Who were the men that visited? What business had they at night in the house of a market trader? My mother's cousin smoked in silence and looked into the distance over the holy man's shoulder as he spoke on in urgent whispers. Now and then, to emphasize some point or other, the holy man would point from where he stood on the narrow stoop towards the sunless inside of our house where I sat unseen, watching and straining to hear. And when my mother's cousin had smoked his cigarette to the butt he broke suddenly from his stillness and put his hands around the holy man's throat and screamed that his business was no one's concern but his and that if the holy man came again to his door he would surely kill him.

Days and nights coiled themselves together. My father did not return to pay my mother's cousin for my keep. But he didn't care; my visitors paid handsomely. Somewhere in the tangle of time, towards spring I think, a policeman came to the stoop. A truck idled on the road, waiting. My mother's cousin raised himself slowly, his eyes wide with alarm. He hissed at me to stay behind the bead curtain. The policeman had a rifle strapped to him; he held it before him, lengthways across his chest, as though to show my mother's cousin the bulk and the weight of it, as though to intimate the damage it could do to the flesh and the bones of his body. I allowed my heart to swell a little with hope. I watched through the beads as the policeman spoke in a flat tone, all the time with the rifle resting on his upturned hands and raised slightly out from him, like a man proffering an infant in church for blessing. But my heart shrank again as he hung his rifle from the nail on the back wall of my tiny room and turned smiling towards me, that familiar hunger lighting his eyes. I heard my mother's cousin's low laugh, the relief in it and the delighted amazement, and the noise of metal scraping on metal as he opened his moneybox.

I stayed in that house until the day my mother's cousin stood burning on the street outside. A tyre had been placed over his head to rest on his broad shoulders and it was doused in petrol and set alight. His hands were tied high behind him. He spun in a small circle for a while. His screams were shrill, piercing; they pained me. The neighbours and the dogs stood still to watch. Some men grinned; others kicked dust into tiny plumes and looked at the ground or sky. Flames licked my mother's cousin's face and melted his eyes. He died on his knees, slumped to one side, his fleshless face melded with the livid wires that remained when the rubber had burnt away. The dogs nosed at him and shrank from the heat. They settled, slavering, to wait.

I walked from the township alone. What worse could happen? Perhaps I hoped I'd be killed. I walked south, away from people. I took a lift in a lorry with a flat bed. Glory, Glory, it said along the wooden side, in white letters. A dove was painted crudely beside the words. I jumped from the flat bed at the edge of a town that had hanging above it a dark cloud, obscuring the sun. The driver pointed towards a mottled window with a door beside it, half opened on a room of shadows. A large woman sat behind a desk. I laughed at the sight of her; it seemed as though the desk grew outwards from her midriff. She appraised me coldly and nodded at an empty chair. Every morning for four years I reported to this fat lady and was told where to go to work. Some days I worked in a factory where plastic delights for children and idiots were pressed from foul gum in great machines, the parts of which could be arranged and rearranged again to make a million shapes. My hands were quick and slender; I was able easily to move the template's edges along routes commanded by a line of red light. Other days I worked in houses, cleaning and caring for white infants whose mothers shopped or talked on telephones. I slept at night in a narrow bed in a long dormitory of other girls and women that stretched like a stem from the back of the fat lady's office. I dreamt often of my family and the village and knew I would see neither again. I dreamt of my father's drowned crop, being rinsed from this earth by the bleeding sky.

I rose one morning and ran, across the world. When I first felt Ireland beneath my feet I was relieved, and tired, and cold. I tasted salt in the wind. The man I work for came to the reception centre in a white van. He sat in it with the engine running and looked towards the main entrance. As people walked from the doors he said English? You speak English? And some of those who did agreed to go with him in the van each night to clean offices and factories. He said, slowly: You'll never be asked, but if you are, say you're an EU citizen. Act offended. If you're asked for proof, say: Do *you* carry proof of your citizenship? That'll fuckin bamboozle them! Then say fuck-all else, only that you're self-employed. All right? Contractors, that's what you all are.

One summer evening he brought me to a house on a narrow street at the end of which there was a small stone church and a graveyard. What do you think of this, Grace? We were at the door of the house. Leave your bucket of tricks there, Grace, you need do no cleaning here tonight. I only want to show you it. Show me what? The house, of course, he said, and laughed, and looked at me. His eyes reminded me of the dogs in the township as they waited for my mother's cousin's body to cool. Would you like to live in this house some day? He gestured about him with his hand, an arcing flourish. He drew out his vowels, like a man whose brain was damaged. He was trying to make me believe him foolish, harmless. There was a garden at the rear of the house, connected to the front by a narrow walkway lined with flowers. The sun pooled on the grass; small white flowers danced in it. Dark evergreens guarded the back wall. I imagined myself for foolish seconds sitting there, unseen, at peace. He gestured again, his hand sweeping out from his chest, like a circus ringmaster. He watched me closely. I thought of Satan, drawing Christ's eyes to the glistening world beneath them, promising, offering to contract. I would live there, and he would have a key. There'd be no peace.

My employer's wife died yesterday. I see him now, standing near the supermarket counter. He has a box of bottles in the crook of his arm. I buy fruit and bread here, humming as I move slowly along the aisles. He is smiling at a well-dressed lady who holds his outstretched hand in both of hers. God rest her, God rest her, the lady is saying. If there's anything we can do for you, anything at all.

She was ill for a long time. He often stood and spoke of her, watching while I worked my way around the empty offices. He'd have a new mop-head to deliver to me, or a bottle of some spray or bleach, as a pretence. It's terrible hard, so it is. Terrible hard to see her that way. Oh, Lord God. My heart is weary, Grace. Go easy, Grace, take your break. Come sit in the van a while. And he'd sit and talk again about the little house and tell me it was mine for only a tiny rent, we could work something out, as soon as I was regularized. Won't it be lovely, Grace?

And he believes in his soul, I think, that it would be lovely. That he would visit at his will and I would smile at him and surrender to him. Just as those boys on the bus this morning thought that I would surrender to their dirty shoes kicking against the back of my seat and their hissed words of spite, their phones descending from above me, flashing and clicking as they stole images of me, to their thin guffaws. I stand still, hidden from his view. He's smiling at the lady; he leaves his hand in hers. His eyes have a light in them, a glint, not of tears but of triumph. This is his victory, he thinks, his time to reap. He's not thinking of the rain.

Retirement Do

I BOUGHT TWENTY Benson from a woman with a shaking hand. She hardly looked at me. Her shop was small and musty, cornered by an empty square. Not long left in either of them, I'd say. I could have done it there, I suppose, but a voice inside said Wait, stick to the plan. I can still see her open shop door from where I'm standing now, spilling darkness onto the bright footpath. There's a stone man above me, someone once heroic or great whose plinth I rest against, and a weeping willow across from me, its branches draped out over a low wall. Caressing the ground, mourning noiseless in the breeze. Lazy, those people, that they wouldn't cut it back. Waiting for the council maybe. There's no cloud at all. Only a fingernail of morning moon interrupts the blue, ragged, like it was bitten off and spat there.

Four cars turned off the main street and parked in the square in the last few minutes. Faces of misery on the people in them. Maybe they've all a funeral to go to. They were all dickied up to the nines, but no colour nor smiles. There's a church there below the road behind the hill I'm nearly sure. There's one somewhere nearby, anyway. I see no spire, but my aspect is low. A woman across the aisle from me on the early bus had a missal and a rosary beads and she tramped off with purpose that way once we got off. This town has a smell about it, like stale milk. A warm breeze sweeps it into my nose. The one smell I hate, I don't know why. I might gag if I had any bit in my stomach. It was the Bensons or something to eat. No contest. Fags take the edge off of hunger anyway.

THERE'S ONLY THE one shade in this town it looks like. Saw him earlier, scratching on the station steps. Fine sugary chops on him. No full-time squad car even, I'd say. Cutbacks. I'd bet he's not the fastest runner, either. He finishes up at five in the evening according to a notice posted on the station door. After that it's your own lookout. You have to tell your troubles into an intercom and a peeler miles distant will sympathize.

I lifted these boots lovely yesterday evening from a gearbag flung down at the edge of a hurling pitch. The lowering sun's dying glare covered me. Old lads training. Junior A or B, jogging red-faced around, short pucks, laughing at each other. I remembered that craic from years ago. Funny how the senior players when too senior get called junior again. It must rankle. Signs on they paste one another vicious. Wallop younger lads for having the cheek to exist. I have the nearly new desert boots of one of them anyway. I was away up the road miles before he panted back to his bag. I left him my old tackies as consolation.

I'm baking now all the same. I might cool myself among that willow's strands. I'm prone to sunburn. My whole head swelled one time so burnt it got, filled with fluid. A tasty little she-doctor lanced it for me free. They have to, you know, if you turn up empty-pocketed. First, do no harm. Harm it would have been to run me unseen to. Foul pus from my roasted crown oozed onto her floor. Not to worry, she said, and smiled, swooping deftly to wipe up. Lord, she was a dinger. Then she read me kindly: melanoma, lotion, stay out of it altogether, cap, and I nodded dumbly, eyes down her front, like a plastic dog on a dingbat's dashboard, placating her.

*

THIS TYPE OF a town polices itself. Squinty eyes in every window. Widow women, risen early, long days to fill with looking; housewives watching for returning children, listening for the squeak of bicycles home safe; well-fed merchantmen protecting their shimmering shopfronts, their patches of footpath swept white. Farms of land outside town, cuteness. Hollow-cheeked tooth-lost wasters at pub doors sucking needle-thin rollups, watching for someone worse or worse off to balm themselves with generous comparison. I have them all well clocked the same way they have me clocked. All I need do now is watch and wait, smoke my fags slowly, each one to the very stub, to the burnt lip. How many will be left when I'm lifted, I wonder?

A swallow hurls itself sunward. High flies, is that a good omen or bad? Small-talk is all omens are. I'll repair to the willow's shade.

I'VE BEEN HERE now, seen and unseen, for a half a morning and most of a deathly afternoon. One slow pass of the time-shared squad is all I've under my belt. Narrow eyes atop a wide face, regarding me darkly. A thick neck bulging over a collar of policeman grey-blue. Working up to it. Those funereal people shuffled back to their cars a good while ago and drove off again stop-starting, rolling slow to join the end of a cortège coming over from behind the hill. I was right, so. Wreaths in the hearse window propped against the coffin sides, twisted into words. Saying: MAM.

More came, parked up, shopped, filled boots, away; no one giving too much regard to the man half veiled by willow tree. I'll have to throw a shape if this keeps up, unplanned for. I'll think on my feet, don't worry. The old one sold me the fags. I've a pain starting in the low part of my back, a hot ache, spreading upwards. I'm getting into bad humour. This footpath unwalked on all day. My sweating fly-bothered holdall unheeded.

I GAVE A GOOD share of my life in England. I never drew social, there nor here. No numbers to my names. Never had a need. Invisible men can't very well appear looking for pensions, though. All a man needs is energy. Once you're careful you're free as the wind. Some people clock for work now with the prints of their fingers. Clockwork people. That's a slippery slope. Pickpocketing at a race meeting: sweets from babies. Confidence tricks: a copybook full of them I had once, scrawled, words and diagrams, unreadable to others. Never go too deep though. Open windows on summer nights in redbrick mansions in silent suburbs. I floated in and out gently with the breeze. Watches, bracelets, necklaces, rings, unlaundered silky things, crisp banknotes. Barely any weight on me. All things easily jettisoned. I slunk unseen like a rat. Watching always for cameras lately, though. They're going to start putting chips into people soon, into their flesh, to track them from space satellites. Plenty old lags already have them over there, clamped to their ankles. Sitting chipped, filling their faces, watching their programmes.

I used to pal about with a few ringdings beyond, when I was very young. We'd smoke on the kerb of the street and watch the respectable people pass. The others would snigger and smirk, I'd only look, and remember. We'd pull a job here and there, nothing major, nothing you'd be remembered for. Day labourers would give us a dark eye passing home, weak with tiredness and hunger, pierced by thirst. Money made for other men with the sweat they dripped into foreign soil. Soaked with it that land, the blood and sweat of Irish sons. Nothing gave to them in return only black livers and rattling chests. Standing bent-backed for their finishes at the thresholds of the giving, pleading for succour with their hangdog eyes and pillowcases of belongings. All pride gone, worked out of them. Living ghosts, looking for a deathbed and a cardboard council coffin. Cap-doffing at heaven's gatepost. Spent.

I lived with an English one for a small while. A bird. Handy. Met her at a bingo hall. I needed a place to lie low and gather myself, and she wanted a clean pet. One of them ones that always needs a fella around, just for the saying of it. Shapely. Rough, though. Council bungalow in a cul-de-sac. Loved television, forever shushing me. One damp day I lamped her close-fisted into the mouth so hard her chin hung swinging from her jaw. Sloppy really, weak, to let that out of me over a bit of shushing, but it fair seared into me for a finish. I took what bit of jewellery she had and forty-nine pounds sterling from a jar in her kitchen cupboard and stepped lightly out of there. I hardly remember now what name I had in that place. Still and all I remember to the pound the amount I lifted from her. Funny the things you log. I often thought to straighten those names I used in my mind. Or am I as well off forgetting them? What's in a name?

A savage slap I gave her, straight out of the blue, blindside. Swelled knuckles after it: stupid carry-on. She had a Superking on the go, halfway to her mouth, her lips pursed for the drag, eyes fixed on the borebox, a shush just finished. She had no notion what hit her. She'd only ever seen the bare smiling shell of me. As she slumped there stupid on the plastic-covered couch, conked, mouth slack, I whispered to her: Now. Fucking shush me now.

I fleeced the lamb, gave her unfeeling tits a grope goodbye and slung my narrow hook. Her Superking's lit end lay smouldering a hole in her shell suit. Cremation. No tracks left. That's no way to behave, though. I'm not proud.

A CURTAIN OF homebound crows draws itself west to east across the sky. Stragglers flap and reel, caw-cawing madly, heavy with corn. Winging I'll bet to that unseen churchyard where they'll roost in trees that hulk darkly, layers of them top to bottom in ancient evergreens, a ranked parliament. Crows everywhere act the same. I wish they'd dip down to me here and pluck the lean corners of me in their black beaks, and carry me skyward. Some sight that would be for the flabby shade, a wing-beaten procession eclipsing his evening.

I'm looking forward to my rest. Thirty-seven years of country lanes behind me; dead weights dragged up soaked and rocky hillsides; slow dissolution of flesh and bones in stinking bubbling limepits; numberless shovelfuls of stony clay dug from sodden wind-wailing moors. I'm crooked from it. Ireland, England, Scotland, Wales. France once. Cursed we are with health, my family, stout unfailing hearts, years to go till death for me. I had a grand-uncle saw a hundred and three. Fell in his garden and the dunt he got killed him. Pink with life till his very last day on earth, rotten with it.

I MADE A GRAB for a little girl a week and a bit ago. Had two small children with her at the entrance to an estate of detached houses. She was brownish, elegant, hair thick and dark. Au pair, I'd say. I had a van with a side-sliding door gaped open, idling obediently, waiting to receive her. Got it from a pavee in Carthy's Cross, plates off a scrapper. She drew back her leg as I dragged her and kicked me full force into the shinbone. The sudden starburst of pain loosened the hold I had on her. The children screeched and shrieked with laughter at the game and ran pell-mell around. She squared up to me, teeth bared. I retreated sharpish, shocked, burnt the van in a woody lane. Standing watching the yellow flames and black smoke swallow it, I decided it was time to finish up. Bested by a slinky girl, my first fail, sore and sorry. I'll do one more or maybe two, I thought, and retire to a concrete box, warm in winter, cool in summer. Three squares and two collations, an hour a day of open air. On my back alone: smoking, thinking, remembering. Desk, paper, biro, books. A television I'll never use. Solitarily confined, the only way to go. Five star.

I bussed it a few days around routes old and new, looping lazily west. I met a girl on a lonely road lined with overlooking trees, a young woman I suppose, walking. Salt in the air, a misty stinging rain blown from the ocean. I looked at her enquiringly and she smiled and stopped to see could she help. Out pounding the roads, minding her shape for her husband. Oh, the lightness in her eyes, the heart-fluttering goodness of her. Softness, shampoo smell, soap and sweat, blonde. I folded her into a ditch after, and sliced a dainty keepsake from her. It's mouldering now in my lightless holdall. Tempted to land it up onto that cop-shop counter and be done. I prefer the wait, though, all considered, the gradual unfolding. To stay still, let circumstances circle me in a fast-decaying orbit till impact. Then a bit of a shemozzle, and I'll rest. Sleep, write a book maybe. An instruction manual. Things will take their course. I hardly hid her at all. She's surely found by now, out in the open, my secret love.

HERE HE COMES at last, hoofing it. Squad's probably gone for the night. Nuisance. I was looking forward to being helped into a soft seat, stretching my legs out before me. Oh, what odds.

Sidling towards me now head back, squinting, lips pursed. Just by the way, like, all casual. Finishing out his shift, cleansing his conscience. He couldn't leave me unspoken to, just in case. No preamble. I like his style. No breath wasted.

What are you at there?

Having my fucking retirement do.

Are you now begod. What's the name?

Jack the Ripper.

Is that right, now. What's in the bag?

Have a look for yourself.

I toe it slowly forward. It grits across the path towards him. He lays a level stare on me, tuts, bends grunting and unzips my muddied holdall with sausage fingers, surprisingly deft. He roots for a few seconds through my tools and bits of clothes and stops suddenly dead, looks sickly, slowly up at me, white-yellow moocow eyes bulging. Her slender hand, cleaved cleanly at the wrist, tumbles indecorously from my bag's gaping mouth and plops palm down on the unyielding concrete. Ah go easy, I tell him, not unkindly. Her solitaire splits the evening light into tiny rainbows. Her wedding band of naked gold looks forlorn and unburnished below it.

He straightens, moaning softly, and stumbles backwards off the shallow kerb, clawing wildly behind himself for balance at the empty air. He lands on his arse with a whump. I turn one-eighty from him calmly, smiling, and stand straight and still, arms obligingly behind, wrists crossed neatly. He'll need a moment or two to regain his feet and his composure. My breath as I speak sways the fronds gently of my weeping willow. A stifled yawn softens my words.

Take me away, and look after me. I'm tired.

Aisling

I ALWAYS SEE something on my half-two fag break. It's the way I have a view out the archway and onto the street. I got a hop there when my eye landed on her, walking in along with her new fella. My hands have pins and needles and I know from them that my heart skipped a beat. I don't know exactly how new the new fella is, but he's newer than me, that's for sure. My oul fella said he spotted her in town during the week all right but I thought he was raving. They're holding hands. The last time she seen me I'd have had a bit more hair and a smaller belly but definitely she would recognize me if I stood out in their path. I'll step back a bit, and let the open door shield me. The new fella looks like a right langer. One of them lads that's all gym muscles, never lifted a block or a keg nor done a proper day's work. She has a summery-looking frock on her, shortish. She always used think she had flaking legs. She had in her hole. They were all right, like. Ah fuck it, they were perfect. They still are.

I seen her cousin a small while ago all right, mooching around in Reception. A big fat yoke she was one time, and she fallen away to nothing. I got a right hop when I recognized her. She's not looking too bad, all the same, tightened up the finest, nothing flapping that I could see anyway. Some of them ones that go right skinny after being mud fat for years do have a fierce sad and sorry look about them. Lonesome after the grub, I suppose. And bits hanging that used to bounce lovely. All the life gone from them. They're waiting now at the front corner near the brasserie side door, her and the fella she's going with a fair old time that won't marry her because he can't decide is he definitely not queer and wants to keep his options open till the very crunch.

They're after clocking each other. I may as well have been a fuckin flowerpot. Squealing and kissing and holding one another out at arm's length like you would a child with a shitty nappy, sizing one another up and letting on they're so fuckin happy to see one another they're having a fuckin orgasm apiece. Every cunt's getting told who's who. The formerly fat cousin's fella is standing with his hands in his pockets, probably keeping a good hold of his langer. No awareness of protocol. Shake the new cunt's hand, you mope. You never seen him before. Ye have been thrown together by the gods of riding. Make the fuckin most of it, you miserable prick. That's all any of us can do.

I hope they don't come into the bar once they've their faces filled. They probably fuckin will, though. She'll be mad for a nose, to see to know am I still here, after all these years. Well, all seven of these years. That's a tenth of a life, or an eleventh, anyway. A twelfth for some long-living cunts. Who'd want to? Looking at telly, dribbling. Thank fuck oul Mossy Bradley got me a grand rectangular badge, solid-golden, with MANAGER wrote across it. I fuckin insisted. Tight prick would have let me write it across my shirt in marker otherwise. I'm going to go handy now with my fag. See can the black lad inside go more than five minutes without making a hames of something.

I can hear it already, and see it, and I know how it's going to go. Matty, she'll say, oh my God, how are you? And *God* and *you* will be stretched to fuckin breaking point. The new fella will stand behind her, smiling, thinking to himself Who's this prick? The cunt'll bristle, like a fuckin Jack Russell, but in that way only men can see. I might come out from behind the bar and give her a kiss and all, and have a grand feel of her, and a smell of her hair, just to spite him. It's great to see you, I'll say, all posh. You look great. Great, great. She'll tell me I look great. Ask how are things. Great, I'll say. Great, great. You're still here, she'll say, and I'll say Sure am, shur where else would I fuckin be? Hahaha! Formerly-Fatarse will smile all fakely and let on she hasn't a clue who I am. I probably won't mention all the nights I seen her in the nightclub here, flubbing around the place, hoping some poor drunken cunt might take her away and try and ride her or rape her or something. Ah, howaya, I'll say, I haven't seen you in years, Jaysus there's fuck all left of you! Or maybe I'll throw a smart dig. I'll see how it goes. The new fella will be told This is an old friend of mine, and I'll think to myself, Ya, old friend, sure. Old friend.

She only got cuntish on me the once. I went for my dinner one day in her parents' house. Mossy gave me the night off especially. I was only gave short notice about the invitation. She picked out what shirt and pants I should wear and all. I arrived a small bit early. I brang you flowers, I told her mother at the door. Oh, the mother says, they're lovely. No smile had she for me. She left the lovely flowers in my hand. I had awful trouble swallowing my food. Not enough gravy, wouldn't please them ask for more. She cornered me after as I came back from the flowery downstairs jacks. I thought for a second she was going to tell me how I was playing a fucking blinder, that the old pair were mad for me. Brang? she said, and a right wicked puss on her. Brang is *not* the past tense of *bring*. *Brought* is. I got a fair old hop. I just remember going What the fuck? Thanks for the fuckin grammar lesson. And deciding there and then she was getting her cards once I'd one more ride got off her. One to remember me by. And something weird happening to my eyes for a second or two. A blurriness, or something, and a stabbing and burning pain in my stomach. But I recovered well and talked away to her oul lad about football the rest of the evening – a grand skin he was – and her mother staying in the kitchen cleaning up, and saying Nice to meet you as I fucked off, and leaving on her sudsy Marigolds the way she wouldn't have to touch off me again.

The black lad is a gas man, alright. As fond as fuck of ones with big arses. No shortage of them around here. He does be in his element here the weekend nights, throwing his eye around the whole night long. He must go home and flog the log off of himself. I'm a kind of fond of the black lad now all the same. He makes a bags of things regularly still, but he's generally sorry and willing to make amends. A rake more of them arrived in here one evening. He was up in an awful heap when he seen them swinging in. Happy, like, and nervous, kind of. Said they were his brothers. But most likely any of them that comes out of the same patch of jungle is called brother. They were all after getting handed student visas and they were as high as kites. Tickets to ride. They were high-fiving my fella and lepping and yoo-hooing out of them in Swahili or some fuckin thing till oul Mossy come out from his crypt and rolled back in the red carpet fair lively. Them lads are nearly as bad as tinkers, he whispered to me, once you give them a welcome the first time they'll have you plagued for evermore. One of them boys around the place is plenty, Mossy says. Looks good, like. The brightness of the smiles of them, you wouldn't believe.

Thinking about that day in her house, though, thinking about it, the oul lad was a funny fish too. I was so happy to be talking shite to him about the Premiership, about which I know everything, and relieved, that I never noticed one or two things properly till after. And you can't trust the remembering of a thing. That's why them airy-fairy cunts say you must live in the moment: it's the only thing that's real. Once a thing passes into history it can be twisted any which way, turned around and upside down. But there was a couple of things, for sure. He must have known I smoked: I seen him clocking the browny-yellow stain along my left index finger before my arse-cheeks landed on their rock-hard couch. But still and all he never asked me had I a mouth on me when he drew his Bensons from his pants pocket. And he got quiet all of a shot once he'd established I was a Penrose. Oh, he says, from the Villas? Ya, you cunt, I felt like saying, from the cunting Villas, what about it? But I said fuck-all only That's right, ya, and I sank back into the old shame that shames me for feeling it. She gave me the road not long after. Off to college, she was. Wouldn't be fair on you, she said.

She made me tall, for two and a half months. I could look any man in the eye. I was king cock. Every prick was jealous of me. I bought her a ring and all, real emerald, off some fuckin hippie at a stall in Galway. She was mad for it. Told me she loved it. Wouldn't even wear it for fear she'd lose it. I got wicked with her a couple of times and put my hand tight on her throat just the once. I seen a mark on her one time that was after all of a sudden appearing and was certain sure it was a love bite. She made out some cunt kicked her on the tit by accident in the pool. He shouldn't of been near enough to your tit to kick it, I told her. I got wicked as fuck. That was the time I caught her by the throat. The fear in her eyes, the look on her lovely face. I'll never in all my days forgive myself.

I cried like a child when she gave me the road. Please, please, don't do this to me. I fuckin begged her. Fuck it anyway, why did I beg? Why in the Jaysus did I cry? Water, bridge, milk, spilt, brokest hearts do be soonest mended. Or some shite. One summer of shifting and riding is all it was. Not even. I was her taste of badness, her little summer work experience, ticked off her list of things to do and have done to her. Like the fuckin chickenpox, she'd only suffer it once.

There was a blemish on the inside of her leg. About the size of a euro. I kissed it one time, and told her it was beautiful. I named it and all, like it was an island I had discovered, a new country. I won't say what I named it. Oh, that's lovely, she told me.

Aisling, her name is.

It means dream. A thing that goes on inside in your head.

A fuckin dream, a dream of fucking.

Maybe that's all it fuckin was.

That's all any of us can do, is dream, and then wake up and face into what's real. The torn things and the slow wait. I'll burn my lip on the last drag of this fag and fuck the remains of it into the bucket. And I'll go back in behind the bar to see what kind of havoc the black lad has wreaked in my absence. And I'll tighten myself a bit and wait.

Crouch End Introductions

I ATE A WHOLE half of a carrot cake last night. I felt funny after it, sugar-sick and weak. My head reeled a tiny bit. I stayed on the couch half asleep till nearly two. Joanie came in all talk from the pub and started wrecking my head so I went to bed. I had bad dreams: a huge dog outside, spiders and snakes inside; I was trapped on the landing, surrounded by barks and hisses and scuttling noises. I screamed in my sleep and woke with a long breath leaving me. I curled up again but couldn't get sleep back. I smoked fags at the front door and watched the brightening of the sky.

Joanie came down about half eleven. There was a stink of drink off her. She was like a lunatic. Some fella did something to her but she wouldn't say what. Tell me, Joanie, tell me, I kept saying to her. Fuck off, you virgin, she said back, what would you know? I never said I knew anything. After a while Joanie laughed a bit and sat clenching her Simon Cowell mug, her fingers twined tightly together, just below her chin. Steam swirled up and blurred her face. Oh, Ellie, she said in a whisper, and smiled at me.

Joanie started into the wine straight after breakfast. She was sloshed before three. I had it in my head to make a proper dinner for me and her and the lodger but then didn't bother once she started into drinking. She put on tapes from the eighties full blast on her big silver time-warp hi-fi. I went down to the basement and looked into the chest freezer for a while at a sirloin joint and thought about defrosting it in the microwave. I could feel the lodger looking at me from the little sofa-bed in the basement bedroom and got cross all of a sudden over nothing. Fuck you, I said into the freezer. I turned and looked at her through the narrow doorway, sitting in the shadows, television light flickering in her eyes. She looked silently back at me. Make your own fucking dinner.

I CAME OVER about two years ago on the Recession Bus. It used to be called the Abortion Bus. Before that joke was thought of it was just called the Bus to London. For those that were desperate. Fifty-five euros. That's some rob. I told your man in the ticket office I was a student. He asked to see my student ID. Show me your mickey and I'll show you my ID, I told him. Fifty-five euros so, he said, and held out his ignorant hand. Here, go on; stick it up in your hole, I told him, as I flung five tenners and a fiver at him. The bus was full and stank of perfume and puke. They squeeze in extra rows of seats to that bus, I'd swear. I'm not tall at all and I was crippled after it. A one in front of me put her seat back to have a sleep. I leaned out over the top of her and said: Put your seat back up. She looked shocked up at me through two innocent blue eyes and said nothing. I kept looking down at her till she straightened. She started reading me in a whisper to her friend. I can hear you, I said, and she stopped.

After I arrived over I spent a good few nights in a doorway with my coat tight around me in front of a statue of a man on a horse. The horse was rearing and the man had a sword drawn. It was summer but still it was cold at night. I walked through the days up and down streets humming with people. Some places had queues that went for miles of people all wanting to see things. I saw a man with loads of different-coloured chalk one day, drawing a picture of Jesus on the footpath. People will walk on him, I said. He's used to that, your man said, and turned back to his picture. I'd say he was a rare holy Joe. I got fed all those days in a redbrick house in a row of other redbrick houses across from a park. There were cobbles on the street outside that hurt my feet through my shoes. Those shoes were only summery things, as thin as tissue. The Salvation Army lived in that house. They ladled soup into white bowls and cut thin sandwiches into triangles and put them on white paper plates and left them out for the lines of ghosts.

All Joanie asked of me the day I sat beside her in the park across from the Salvation Army's house was if I was pregnant. I told her no and asked her for the loan of a fag. She laughed and lit it for me. She told me she needed a girl to help her around the house. I told her no problem and we got three tubes and a bus to her house in Crouch End. A man ran shouting that day along the platform in the second tube station with no shirt or shoes on him. People plastered themselves against the wall as he swished past barefooted, chasing something invisible. The next day Joanie asked me would I mind hoovering her two front rooms and the hallways up- and downstairs. Then after a few weeks she asked me would I mind giving an old man a few slaps across the arse, and if I didn't mind I could stay indefinitely and would need to pay no rent. I told her no problem but that I'd go no further than that. She showed me what to do the first day while the old man bent over the back of a leather chair with his white arse cocked up in the air waiting, his well-tailored trousers pulled down to his knees.

Look, a short throw of your wrist, try to get him evenly across both cheeks. Joanie blistered him with a long narrow switch and then handed it to me. The old man moaned while I reddened him. I skin him now twice monthly, and a handful of others.

They normally fix up with Joanie, and never a geek out of them about it. I don't know do they even get a horn.

MY FATHER RAN off when I was seven or eight with a lady two doors down who had boobs like beach balls with half the air gone out of them. She had yellow hair and black eyebrows. She always wore black leggings and was forever pulling her knickers out of the crack of her arse. She gave him the road before too long and took up with a black fella. My father gave himself over to drinking cider from plastic flagons in an archway off Catherine Street. His body is still there, swallowing cider, but his soul is long gone from him. That can happen to people, you know, without them even realizing it.

I made up my mind to bus it to London the day I looked up from the kitchen sink and saw through the window my brother folded against the back wall with his two arms wrapped around himself and his mouth open in the shape of a scream. He was dying of the pain inside in him. His eyes were closed tight but his face was washed with tears. He's beautiful, my brother. All the things that happened him, that were done to him. He was crouched down there in a clump of weeds and high grass, keening like a banshee for the things that were taken from him, or never given him, or something, something. His good grey hoodie was stained and frayed at the elbows and his jeans were walking with the dirt. His white runners were turned black. I remember well the day he bought those jeans and runners to wear to his FAS course. He was as proud as anything. Four shades who'd been chasing him burst in through the back gate and grabbed a quarter of him each and lifted him stretched and screaming away.

I had to get my stuff and leave that day so that I'd never again have to bear helpless witness to such sorrow. Looking at my brother's pain was like being stabbed and stabbed. My beautiful brother. I wonder how is he now. I wonder how the boy is he stabbed in the stomach the night before the morning he jumped the wall into our garden and crouched doubled over on himself in agony while I stood unseen at the kitchen window looking out at him, my heart shredding itself to ribbons. My mother reached for me that day and I pushed her backwards away from me. She landed sobbing on her hands and knees on the kitchen floor. The sight and the sound of her turned my stomach sick. Her sunken mouth and eyes, her sorrow for herself. You done that to him, Mammy, I said. Cathal, my Cathal, she bawled, reaching upwards for her fags. I walked on the splayed fingers of her other hand as I left.

Mammy took up with a good few yokes in the years after Daddy ran off. None of them was any great shakes, and one of them was the devil. I took Mammy's children's allowance book from her locker drawer the day I left and went to the post office. The girl at the counter didn't even look up as she handed me over the notes. Then I walked out the short mile to the county home and sat beside the devil for a while in a ward that smelt of shit and soap. The devil hasn't the use of himself any more; he was struck by a stroke a couple of years ago, the one favour God granted me.

I went to the kitchen and asked a girl there could I have a pot of tea. I told her I was okay for cups. And I walked back to the devil's bedside and pulled back the covers of his bed and lowered his grey pyjama bottoms gently by the string and poured the tea carefully onto his wrinkly purple prick. His body kind of shuddered, his eyes bulged like a cartoon man's, his mouth gaped so wide I thought the skin at either side of it would tear. His wild eyes turned to me and I smiled. Don't tell anyone, sure you won't? I whispered into his tufty ear. Be sure and keep this little secret the way Cathal and me always kept yours. I covered him up again and blessed myself and left. Thanks for that, I said to the girl in the kitchen as I handed her back the teapot. You're welcome, sweetness, she said back.

JOANIE RANG THE Chinese around seven. What will I get for the lodger? I told her I didn't know. Oh, fuck a duck. I'll just get three sweet and sours and three chips. The lodger poked a ratty nose through the basement door when she heard the telltale revving of the delivery scooter. I shoved a plastic box of sweet and sour chicken and a bag of chips at her. Then I felt kind of sorry and shouted down along the darkness for her to come and eat with us in the kitchen. Is okay, she shouted back up and I got suddenly cross again and slammed the basement door. Joanie spilt sauce all over her leg and she screeched in pain. I went to help her wipe it off and she grabbed my wrist and squeezed it hard. Get your fucking stinking Irish hands off me, you little *bitch*, she hissed at me. Fuck you, Joanie, I said back, and she slapped me hard underneath my eye. Her ring opened my skin. That'll be the day that *you* fuck *anything*, Joanie said through her down-turned mouth before she started to shovel balls of battered chicken into it. I left her at it. *X Factor* was starting anyway.

Ellie, Ellie, I'm sorry, Joanie said as she splashed onto the couch beside me. You know, don't you, that I love you, don't you, my doll? And she stroked the side of my face with her soft hand before slumping snoring against me. I quenched her fag and prised her wineglass from her manicured fingers and arranged her more comfortably before moving to the armchair for *Xtra Factor.* I heard a series of soft creaks from the stairs and then the sound of the pipes clanking and groaning as the shower came on.

I felt an urge to go to the kitchen and run the hot tap full bore to freeze her little arse but resisted it. That'd be horrible. I was fair tempted, though. One of the other lodgers months ago was tall and dark-skinned. I put a fresh dogshit from the path outside into her bed once while she showered; I scooped it up into a plastic bag and left it under her duvet, halfway down the mattress. Then I lay in bed and wondered why I'd done that. She never mentioned it. Her Paki came and took her the following week and left an envelope fat with cash for Joanie. I went and checked and the shit was as I'd left it. She must have seen it and slept on the floor.

The doorbell rang. I saw a hulking shape through the side blind of the bay window, hunched at the top step, as though poised for something. Joanie snorted and stirred. Whassa, whassa, she asked, lifting herself. Her skirt was riding up over her hips, her black knickers on show. They looked expensive. The shape outside was standing still, and some cold wind blew through me, and it brought a smell of ashes, a warning smell.

As Joanie wobbled around the room looking for her shoes I slipped upstairs and waited on the landing. Ellie, Ellie, answer the fackin door, she was screeching in her true Cockney, ANSWER THE FACKIN DOOR! The doorbell rang again and I heard her cursing and fumbling with the lock. ELLIE! All fackin right, will you just . . . and the hulking shape was in the hallway, and there was a violent shuffling, a muffled screaming, and there was a noise like a football being bounced hard on wet grass, over and over again. I stood by the banister, gripping the top rail, staring at the whiteness of my knuckles, and then at the wide-eyed lodger, haloed by steam in the bathroom door, a towel tight around her middle. Silence suddenly fell and after long empty seconds we heard the sound of a man crying softly. Oh, Mum, he sobbed. And the door clicked gently closed. There are only so many stories in the world.

I've left Joanie lying in the hallway for tonight. I only had one bare glance at her. She's dead all right, because her glassy eyes are facing the foot of the stairs and her body is towards the front door. It's black flagstone, thank God, easily cleaned. There isn't much blood anyway. I wonder will the lodger help in the morning. If she doesn't offer I won't force her. That'd be lousy. She'll have to give me a hand getting Joanie into the chest freezer, though. For all her minding of herself there's a fair old heft to Joanie.

And soon the lodger's Paki will come and leave a bulging envelope for the proprietress of the Crouch End Introductions Agency. But right now I have half of a carrot cake to eat and tomorrow there's a freezer to be filled and a white and ancient arse to be whacked.

Meryl

IT WAS JACK MATT-AND told us the story of what happened the night a girl from the Villas wiped eyes and broke hearts, bringing down the house as Pegeen Mike in *The Playboy of the Western World*. Jack Matt-And was there that night, at the back of the hall, swaying.

Jack Matt-And was so called because he'd start every sentence with And. He'd arrive in already drunk and he'd drink away steady and seem to get no drunker, but he'd sit at the end of the bar telling stories of other times he was drunk, in a soft chant that'd kind of lull you into listening. Like this he'd go:

And I was on Church Road. And I had only one shoe. And one leg of my pants was drowned wet. And my left eye was closed and wouldn't open. And my mouth was scalded with pain. And the yard of the church was lit white by the moon. And the sapless old trees loomed along it. And Our Lord and His saints were asleep inside. And a man walking down towards the gate in a coat that was tied at the front and pinched inwards looked down at the ground and then up at the sky, and adjusted his path to avoid me. And I was prostrate like a penitent dog who was kicked from a house that he'd shat in. And the man hummed a tune through his thin bloodless lips so the air wouldn't be still between us. And he could pretend this was something he saw every time he walked out through the moonlight.

*

HER REAL NAME now is only an echo of an echo in the town. That's how hard the nickname fastened itself to her. Meryl. As in Streep. Her people were nothing to boast about. Her father was Paddy Screwballs, who was left go from the buses over something only whispered about. Something not known about so it by default became something terrible, and shameful. Sure it must have been. She had one brother a labourer, big-fisted and dark, and another brother who wasn't all there who went down to Roscrea every day on the free bus to the funny farm, and a sister who was gone years, married to an English fella. Her mother was dead a good long while, from some unnamed thing only women get.

I gave the spaces between orders to looking at her. Go on away and pull yourself, Bofty told me one time. You're no good to me with your balls bursting full. You'll be spilling drink and giving out wrong change and making a pure solid hames of things. And he rested his belly on the draining-board of the glasses sink inside the bar and rested his eyes on Meryl. You always got the feeling she didn't know how lovely she was. You always got the feeling she couldn't feel you looking.

When you're young and quiet and you move around softly and keep your eyes cast mostly down it's easy to hear things. People forget you're there, or forget you might hear, or don't care if you hear. I was finished up with school and I hadn't a great Leaving Cert got and my father was at me daily to go into the buildings, there was a power of money to be got in the buildings, there was lads hadn't hands to wipe their arses clearing five or six hundred pounds a week. Imagine what the lads in the pantses and shirts and white helmets get! And they only required to stand around the place looking at bits of paper. But I liked the pub and the hum of talk and the safety of knowing where everything was and what everything did. And I liked the looks I got through windows opened by drink into the realness of people.

I often thought of a poem from school when she was in the bar. The one about the planter's daughter. Men saw her, and drank deep, and were silent. Or sometimes they were the opposite of silent, but it amounted to the same thing: they dribbled and spat words everywhere, and tried to be funny, in a panic of desire. And when she wasn't there, people talked about her, and I listened.

She wasn't from land, or from anything. She had no right swanning about the place the way she did. She had no right going up near the tennis club or into the dramatic society, dragging trouble after her. She had no right going with Felim Hackett to Junior Chamber meetings, and sitting up at the front smiling at all the men. What commerce was ever done in the Villas? The quare kind, that's all. She had no right getting cast as Pegeen Mike by the professional director the dramatic society brought in to make a right good job of *The Playboy of the Western World* for their centenary. They couldn't dissuade him. Oh, the money that was spent on that man and that's what he did to them! That's the thanks they got.

It was a given thing Noreen Keogh would play Pegeen Mike in the centenary year. It was her great-grandfather, a doctor, who had started the society. Her grandfather had taken the mantle of it, and both her parents had trodden those worn and hallowed boards, and they used to be beautiful together. Wasn't it a fright to God the way that one blew in and wagged her chest in that Dublin fella's face and stole the part off of poor Noreen? But it was the great-granddad had done the damage. It was he drafted the society's constitution and the rules laid down there had been adhered to for a century and a person given casting power in a properly constituted meeting of the society by a majority of members could not be overruled. And they had that power given to the fancy-pants director from Dublin they as good as emptied their coffers for the way their centenary production would be something special, to be remembered across the ages. But it had been unspoken yet agreed by all that Noreen Keogh would play Pegeen Mike. It had been made clear. It had, it had.

They did their damnedest to get out of the contract with the director. The Foxes even took it to the owner of the chip-shop franchise they'd bought into. He's a great man for contracts. And advice. Like never pay a person the same wages two weeks in a row. Put fuck-all in writing bar what's laid down by law. Don't mind that public holiday bollocksology. Always pay in cash. Let nobody ever get cosy on you.

HERE'S MERYL STREEP! someone shouted in here on opening night, as she walked through the door, and that was it. It went from a compliment to a jibe even before that night was over. *Meryl*, Noreen Keogh's crowd would sneer, and laugh without mirth. It stuck. Within weeks her transcendent performance was forgotten and Meryl was stuck on her as a tag of ridicule. Is that her real name? outsiders would ask. No, someone would say, she was gave a part in a play one time and it went to her head! Hahaha! And that was how they took back from her what they believed she'd had no right to. That was the revenge they exacted. She was never again known by her God-given name, only by Meryl, and it wounded her, I knew by her eyes, because of the way it was said, and the feeling of foolishness that became attached to it, and the strong hint of spite that was always there in the saying of it.

Paddy came in with her to the bar on that opening night. It wasn't too long after the smoking ban came in. Between that and the fact that he'd never before strayed from Collins's snug, he wasn't in the full of his comfort. He must have got carried away with his pride in her, the sudden break in his fallings of rain. I watched him from behind the taps, smiling, nodding at people, letting on to be grand. I could see the redness rising slowly up his neck, the beads of sweat on his brow, the way he scratched himself without knowing he was doing it. I watched him try to stand a round of drinks for his daughter and her new friends. I saw the shake in his hand, the fifty tight inside in it. But she was busy being congratulated, and Felim Hackett who played Christy Mahon opposite her didn't hear him asking, and the director fella with the paisley waistcoat and the roundy glasses didn't hear him either, so close in conversation were they, and he put his hand on the arm of a man I didn't know too well, an accountant with an office near the castle demesne, and asked him what was he having, and the man just looked down at Paddy's hand, and muttered he was in a round, thanks. And old Paddy reached for his fags, and caught himself, and took the excuse to slip out the back door and keep going, across to Collins's where he belonged. I heard her asking Felim Hackett where her dad was gone a while later. Felim only looked at her and turned down the corners of his mouth and shook his head.

Paddy never heard Jack Matt-And's recounting of the play. Paddy never felt the change in the air after it, the thickening, the seeping hate.

And on she came. And Lord she was lovely. And she made those oul lights seem like sunshine. And not even a breath could you hear. And never before did I see such a thing, the way the whole hall fell away. And there was only that girl on the stage there before me, and only her voice could I hear. And that now I know is what's meant by transported, for she took me right out of that place. And never before in one hundred years was there beauty like hers on that stage.

And on he went, eyes closed, in a rapture. Ah shut the fuck up, Noreen Keogh's first cousin said, and a few laughed and a few more sighed. But there was nothing now could be done. She gave Jack Matt-And a kiss when he'd finished his recital and she stepped outside of herself and became Pegeen Mike, every night for a week. This was no amateur dramatics, she could have been on Broadway. Bofty had put up a right dinky smoking shed in the back yard, open-sided but still cosy, with a free-standing stove in the centre of it. I went out there one night not long after the play finished up and saw Felim Hackett talking to her in an angry whisper, jabbing a lit cigarette towards her face, and she was saying nothing back, just sitting straight-backed on her stool, her eyes bright with tears, an unlit fag in her right hand, her left hand out towards him, palm up, as if in surrender. I saw them shifting that night in the doorway of Bridgeton's Hardware, one of his hands clamped tight to her arse, the other on the back of her neck, curls of her blonde hair entwined in his fingers. He gave her the road not long after and got engaged to a farmer's daughter from up around Lackanavea side that had a job in the Galway Clinic as a radiographer or radiologist or something starting with radio.

She took up with a fella from Limerick for a finish, rough-looking enough, shaven-headed, cocky. He had a swanky car. One of them lads. She moved away, to God-knows-where, somewhere she could have her name back, and she was only seen back for Paddy Screwballs's funeral. And the air in the bar was normal again, even without the smoke.

Royal Blue

I GOT THE IDEA off a big fat tinker. He took the council for millions. I wanted no millions, only enough, and a bit more for a cushion. I walked up to Walter's Lane the same night I seen his story in an *Evening Herald* I lifted off a café table. I wanted to see a king in the flesh. The campsite was at the end of acre after acre of horses and scrapped cars. He was staggering around like a man on a ship's deck in a rolling sea; there was drink glopping out of a bottle in his massive hand, there was a bonfire behind him, a halo all round him. He was the same as Our Lord to them people, what he done for them, the riches he brought them, the salvation. They danced around him in a ragged ring, screaming and roaring and laughing. He got them a home, too, that they didn't even want. He was drowning in glory. He eyeballed me as I stood at the entrance staring in; he bared his yellow crooked tinker's teeth and I turned and ran as his people's quick eyes fell on me. My ma was an Amazonian, or something. I run wicked fast.

Mary Heffernan came and got me when I was eleven. Time for you, Heffer, I said. Heffer, I always called her. Cow wasn't none too pleased. Called her it the whole time, every time I seen her. Ah, howya, Heffer, I'd go, and the odd time I'd throw in a moo or two for good measure. She dragged me down the concrete steps from the flats that first time, Da following behind, keening out of him, drink-breath wafting from him. Jaysus, Da, will you relax, I told him. Cop on to fuck, you're not able to look after me. He was roaring how he loved me and I was all he had as Mary Heffernan strapped me into a booster seat in the back of her tiny car. HSE rules an all. I'm a tall girl now, leggy, but I wasn't quite one point five metres that time. Rules is rules is rules.

My ma got deported before I could walk. Sometimes I think I remember her, but it's probably just a dream I'm remembering, or a picture I have of her made of Da's memories. I don't know how she and my da made me. It must have been like a lioness getting mounted by a mangy oul tomcat. Loads a them wans done that, Da told me. Come over an rode the first poor bollix they seen. Trying to get up the pole to get a passport. But something went wrong with the plan, he said. He wasn't ever great on specifics. They got some hop the day they come for her, he said, when they seen she was actually there, waiting for them! She told him don't worry, she'd be back in a few weeks. Right in front of the coppers an all. They only rolled their eyes and asked did she need help with her bags. She spat on the ground at their feet and walked down all them steps with her suitcase balanced on her head, just to spite the fuckers. Lift wasn't even busted that time. Elegance of her, Da would say, making the wavy shape of the outline of her in the air with his hands. Like a fucking queen. Like a fucking queen. Lord God, he fair loved her. He loved telling me that story. I took what I got.

I got put with a family in Blacksmith's Walk, down at the shady end of the East Wall. I had it in my head I'd get a fucking Barbie if I got in with a real family for a while. I hadn't bargained on how much I'd miss my da. Started crying for him an all, first night out. That crowd had only sons, two smelly yokes, looking at me with hungry eyes. Keep them boys away from me, I told the woman of the house once Heffer had fucked off to chew the cud somewhere. Her oul fella laughed and smiled at me kindly but she showed me no gentleness. Called me *young lady* the whole time. Any fuckin Barbies, missus? I asked her, through my tears. She had no way at all about her, that one. She wasn't bad, I'd say, but she sure wasn't good either. A big nothing, sucking the cash for giving hot meals and warm beds and cold shoulders to the children of people from a few cuts below her. Put her hand on me roughly once or twice. I legged it after less than a week. Them manky-looking small fellas gave me the creeps. Snotty and silent, they were. Animal eyes. Probably rapists by now.

I learnt all the streets' twists and turns and sometimes when the cold stung me too much I'd turn myself in for a while. No house could hold me long. I first seen the house on a stint I done in the wild when I was fifteen. I had found Da that day, thrown down at the foot of the spire, nearly expired. I got all choked up over the bollix. There was a vulture or two circling, swooping, their shadows moving in and out around him. Someone got him on the junk, smacked him up, strung him out. He probably thought he had to. Probably apologized to the dealers for not getting on the hard stuff years ago, for never having given them a turn. I dragged him up the street as far as the Garden of Remembrance and plonked him on a bench and slapped him and kissed him and cried tears over him that stung my eyes coming out. And I left him there to burn in the afternoon sun, protected by a small army of Japaneses armed with cameras as big as their heads.

The house was only ever meant to be a temporary thing, a place to put my da a while, the way he'd be out of the eye-line of the vampires that wanted his dole money and whatever he made from the robbing and the welfare strokes in exchange for packets of dust that they hid in the cracks of themselves. There was a long narrow jungle to the back of it, grass the height of my chest, twisted crab-apple trees, giant rhubarbs, a tiny toilet in a broken shed that must have been for servants one time. There was running water, somehow, but no juice. Da came clean of the gear after a terrible fortnight of screaming and sweating and vomiting and had wits enough back to lift a car battery and a circuit breaker and a coil of wire and a few other bits, and we were able to listen to the radio and run a tiny fridge that was got from the Clarion Hotel. We had a camping stove and sleeping bags and some pots and pans and a knife and fork each and all that summer we were cosy and happy. That's when I seen the story in the *Herald* about the tinkers.

The house was a three-storey redbrick island in a sea of grey concrete and wild grass. Boarded and crumbly but built for the centuries. There was nothing in front only road, and nothing behind only field that stretched away to a hump with a posh school beyond it. You could often hear roars and shouts of matches being played coming across the breeze. There was a petrol station with a shop to the left as you stood at the door, across a half-acre of scrub, and a pylon and a mast in a fenced-off square to the right. I often wondered was it healthy to be living in the shadow of that yoke. Then I'd think again about what healthy was, what good for you meant, what bad for you could mean. Da done a powerful job that late autumn, his crowning glory, the best thing he ever done. He dredged up his talent from where it had lain soaked in the dark inside of him and painted a mural on the downstairs walls of the inside of the house, of a line of children, dancing, running, happy, being led along a flower-strewn path towards a forest, by a tall, slender woman with a suitcase on the top of her head, and her arms out a bit from her sides, her long fingers beckoning to the children behind. Then he bust in one night to the shop and run a sealed wire out from it and along the back wall and through the scrub and into our house and we had proper power. And he sat at the end of that week of work in the glow of a bulb and the flickering television light, warmed by a three-bar heater and he smiled and looked along his line of painted children and up at his painted Amazonian love and said Now, sweetheart, didn't I do something? And I kissed him on his rough forehead and said Yes, Da, you surely did.

A fella from the shop copped us. He spotted Da's tidy drill-hole and the plastic-covered wire run out from it and followed it along the wall and the scrub and through our back fence and up the crab-apple forest to the back of our house. He burst in through the back door I had only barely barred. Da was out, doing a bit. He had a bulgy belly and bulgier eyes and wet lips. But still an all there was a kind of a pleasantness about him, or something. Jaysus, wha? I asked him. I'll pay you for the juice, sir. He only stood looking, licking his tacher with a darting tongue. I read him like a fuckin book. The second time he come I recorded it on a digital camera Da picked up somewhere, perched and aimed on a high shelf, and the third time I played it back for him and he nearly shat himself. I have copies made of that, too, I told him, and he went from pink to white to purple and I thought he might fall away in a heap, dead. Ah here, I told him, go easy, just drop us in a bag of messages once a week and look after my da's wire and we'll all stay friends. And the years rolled on and bit by bit we lined our nest, my da and me.

I walked back up to Walter's Lane last night, just for the one look, to see were they still there, or people like them at least, cousins or clansmen or something. There was houses there now, low affairs, chalets, I think they're called. There was cars and vans, big ones. No sign of the king, or his band of followers. A dog stood sentry near the same gateway I looked in from twelve years ago. We won't go as wild as them people did, Da and me. We'll probably be in the papers the same way, the solicitor has me told, people do go mad for these rags-to-riches tales, these adverse possession stories, squatters getting given proper rights. The untitled, the unentitled, getting gave title. The poor becoming rich at the stroke of a pen, the fall of a judge's hammer, because rules is rules is rules. Land is a finite resource, he says, and the courts abhor its waste. Da will be a king tomorrow, and I'll be a princess, and we'll take the boards from across the front door of our castle and we'll sand it and paint it a deep royal blue.

A Slanting of the Sun

I KNEW WELL that boy hadn't it in him, from the very first second. Every part of his face and head was covered by a black mask, bar his eyes and mouth. It was his eyes gave him away. I knew he was young by the cut of him: the legs of his tracksuit pants tucked into his socks, the bit of bum-fluff I could see sprouting through the pimples above his lip. I could hear Michael crying inside in the kitchen; they had him dragged in there from his room and he sitting up straight and tied with a rope to the back of his chair and his hands up high behind him. The noise of him was cutting and slicing through the air. I was lying on my side at the top of the stairs without the power of myself, and the boy was standing half the way up the stairs so that our eyes were about level. Mine were sideways and full of tears; his were the right way up and shining. With fear, and something else, I didn't know then what. Drugs, I supposed, in that first moment. I had a fair dig already got from one of the fellas that had turned over my room and dragged me out as far as the landing and were now interrogating my brother. I could just make out the side of Michael and the pose of him in the chair. All I could think as I looked at him was: That's the straightest he's sat in donkey's years. And there was me and that young lad, facing one another, and both our hearts crossways.

Michael and myself had nearly that whole evening given over to composing an ad for the *Ireland's Own*. God, we had great sport doing it. We had the finished article left on the sitting-room sideboard, folded in two, awaiting an envelope. Several drafts were balled up inside in the recycling bin. Several more were burnt in the fire. Michael was kind of embarrassed starting off the writing of it, but once he settled into it he knocked great fun out of it. Lord almighty, says he, what'll land up to the door? I'd say now you'll have to meet the first time in a hotel lobby or something, I told him. Oh, says he, sure yes, of course. And he nodded and smiled at the thought of it, and removed and replaced his spectacles several times in quick succession, and rubbed his cheeks in pleasant nervousness.

I think this is near enough word-for-word what we decided on for a finish for Michael's ad.

> Bachelor farmer, retired, quiet, mannerly, respectful, RC, NS, SD, Mid-west, own car, early sixties, likes walks, country and western music, some dancing, WLTM similar lady of any age, preferably younger, for friendship and maybe more.

RC is Roman Catholic. NS is non-smoker. SD is social drinker. We got them from a little box at the bottom of the page of personal advertisements. Michael said wasn't it a pity we had no computer, the way we could send off the ad by the email. I allowed it was, if only to save paper. What about it, says Michael, probably we're as well off. Those yokes only draw trouble. I wasn't sure what he meant by that. But I agreed away all the same and he went off to his bedroom across the hall smiling and I stayed up and smoked two or three more fags and listened to the murmur of him saying his prayers.

There was a silence inside in Michael, like a space where nothing existed. A hole, kind of, or more than that. A vacuum, isn't it, where an empty space hasn't even air in it? Some would just say it was loneliness, a longing for a sharing of his days with someone besides his older brother. More would contend he had a want in him. He did, but not in that way that they meant. He was forever trying to fill it in, cover it, with prayers and going to Mass and helping out in the parish and what have you. Night after night he gave whispering up at God, reams of words written by saints and holy men, imagined things, if only Michael knew. I'd never have disabused him of his holy notions, but I knew the hollow centre of those things, the untruth of the Word that gave him such comfort, the conceit that was attached to it, invisible to Michael and his fellow believers.

I often walked the road home with vicious thoughts bent into the shape of my mind. Of women with tight skirts hiked up and bunched at their hips, bent forward before me, and torn stockings and redness in their faces from a mingling of pain and longing and I'd cut over across the bottom meadow to the stream and stand in the ruts of the tracks of cattle hard from frost and look into the water and up at the sky and wonder why such torments invaded me. Why such natural thoughts turned in me to such unnaturalness, why any god would create a creature such as me. It was those days that the truth of myself and of wider things started to come creeping clearly to me: that there was something twisted and cruel existing unwanted inside in me; that the world had neither god nor devil in it or over it; that humankind wasn't commanded or battled over or even thought about by any divine or lowly thing but we were all only accidents of the meeting of flesh, flesh wrought from the meeting of tiny things wrought by a chance slanting of the sun, things without meaning or rhyme.

From this remove now I can consider those moments on the night of the robbery far more clearly than before. I don't shake as much from the recollecting and my breath doesn't catch and turn jagged in my throat so that I feel I might suffocate. There was a shadow all the time after on the wall and floor that seeped back out through the paint and the plaster. Where the blood of my brother splattered and splashed. A young cousin of mine scraped off the old paint that had the blood on it and sanded the wood of the floor and varnished it and laid new paint on the wall. And back came the shadow through the new paint and varnish. So my cousin took away the old plaster and took up the boards of the floor and re-plastered and re-floored and still the shadow rose through from below and when I told him he just put a hand on my shoulder and looked into my eyes not unkindly and I saw in his face the certitude of my madness. I could nearly hear him telling his wife: Poor Alphonsus. He's gone as mad as a brush ever since. Ever since. And their thoughts must surely then have turned unbidden to my fallow fields and the uncoined worth of them and the subvention that might be available to them for the new nursing home away over in Lackanavea.

The Kilscannell Robbery, it came to be known as. Talked about like a story, a made-up thing, a sort of a legend. It sounds like the name of a Western said that way. The Kilscannell Robbery. And isn't that really all it is, a story? It only exists inside the heads of people; it can't be grasped or touched, only rendered in guesses and surmises, people saying *I'd say* this and *I'd say* that. And for me it's a story too, of Michael's terrible ending and of that young lad and how he looked at me and the pain in him as he watched me watching down along the stairs and through the kitchen door as a hulk of a man with a familiar darkness in him drew back his hand again and again and roared and screamed the same question over and over in time with his blows. Where's the money, where's the money, where's. The fucking. Money. The Credit Union, Michael whispered with the tail-end of his breaths; it's all inside in the Credit Union, every penny, and he said he was sorry, sorry, sorry and he slumped forward as far as their binding of him would allow and he died there in his bloody pyjamas in the hard high-backed chair he'd bought in as part of a set in hope or expectation of the arrival into our home of someone who'd appreciate or admire such things.

And I wished the paralysis would lift from that masked boy and that some fountain of anger or strength or badness or desperation would spout from within him and empower his arm to bring down upon me his weapon, the hooked thing in his hand, the wheel-brace or toothed crowbar or whatever it was he held – I only saw it through the blurriness that veiled my eyes whenever I turned them away from my brother. Sort out the other cunt, one of his mates had shouted to him, and he'd come all shapes the halfway up the stairs to meet me, prostrate on the landing. He never knew his own soul until that moment; I saw the knowing descend on him. He never knew the distance between the imagining of violence and the doing of it.

The only movement of him I could see was a trembling. Even his eyes were still, but shining all the while. The leader of them hadn't yet laid into Michael, and the thought about the strange sight of the straightness of Michael's poor back was still fresh and foolish in my head and all of a sudden I knew all there was to be known about that boy. It was the very same as if I was looking into a mirror that reflected only what was inside of a person. I was visited by a new kind of clearness I had never once possessed in all my days. Maybe that's the way of epiphanies: that a man must be at his most desperate before they bless him. Not that I counted myself blessed in that moment, lying without the power of my legs or control of my bladder, with no defence, at the mercy of madmen, and a child before me being chased by the Fates towards a precipice.

I was never able to do the things that I thought of doing inside in my head. I never had the boldness to close my hand on twisting chance. Whenever the wind blew right for my desires I hadn't my sails set. I was resolute in my unpreparedness: designedly I sat becalmed and drifted, away from opportunity. I knew myself. But this same self-knowing that I gained in sorry increments over a lifetime was descending all at once on this boy as he stood on our ancient stairs, though what he was all of a sudden coming to see inside himself was different from what I had discovered inside in me. There's a lot to be said for an eventless existence all the same, where knowledge can be gradually gained, examined and tested at leisure, coped with and brought more easily to terms. While standing in a high meadow burning gorse, or looking at a hurling match, or watching from a distance the bare shoulder of a woman and the thin line left white where a strap of some garment had held off the sun. A slow, drawn-out facing of the truth, a lifetime of gentle revelation.

But no such ease for this boy. He was being crushed under the weight of his discovery. He knew now in this sudden stillness on the stairs of the house my father's father built that he wasn't like his savage comrades: he hadn't what he saw as their strength, their bravery, their careless fists; he wasn't able to look with derision on an old man lying in his own water with his mouth opening and closing in silent pleading and spit on him and beat from him the whereabouts of balls of imagined money. And he had only seconds left before he had to separate his back from the wall that had been thrown up unexpectedly behind him and if I'd had my voice I'd have told him, Don't worry, son, you are who you are, go on back down to the scullery and take down the biscuit tin from the top shelf that's tucked in behind a load of empty marmalade jars and there's a Visa card in there and the number of it is nine-seven-nine-oh and you can draw out as much as you want out of it and won't that placate the other two and you can buy yourself a bit of time that way to put distance between yourself and this life you're trying to make yourself live and you can go somewhere and be good, the way whatever set of chances that brought you into being meant you to be.

What design is there, though? The killing of Michael started then and still the boy stood and flinched each time a roar sounded followed by a wet thud and after a long few moments he looked back over his shoulder and the borders of flesh I could see around his eyes and mouth were paler again when he turned back and the trembling of him was even in his legs. And the dark man was in the hall now and his comrade was a shadow behind him and I couldn't make out what he was screaming up at us for the loudness of it but I think it was Do him, do him, do him to fuck will you, do him, and I saw the boy's lips move in the shape of I'm sorry and a tear fall from each of his blue eyes and his arm swing back and over his head and down and the night came falling in.

And when all that was done and they were gone and I rose out of that darkness, I tried to move myself to untether my brother and lay him down the way he'd be respectable-looking, the way he'd wish to be, but I hadn't the strength to crawl from beneath my blanket of pain and it was the end of the morning before my cousin came in through the door and found Michael dead and me not far from it. And I couldn't bide long with that shadow haunting my days and for a finish one frosty morning some tiny dam inside in my head gave way and the workings of my arms and legs and tongue were drowned in blood and I was carried here to this home and I won't stir too far from this bed again until they carry me to the flat-roofed mortuary that's appended to this place, itself like an unmoving limb.

My carer comes in here even on the days he's not down to be working at all. He doesn't let on at all but I know. I heard that shrieking shrew of a matron one day and she interrogating him outside in the corridor. What in the name of Jesus do you mean, coming in here and you not rostered on? Well, I was doing nothing else and I kind of promised Mister Reilly I'd stay going with that book we're reading. And she tutted and huffed and shot something at him about how he needn't think now he'd be getting paid for it and no overtime had been approved by Upstairs and he said Oh God no, I'm here as a visitor, and she clomped away, still giving out as she went.

And as he reads, slowly, stumbling on the odd word, I feel relief that he's here, and a joy I never felt in all my days, and a peacefulness, and I allow myself the warm foolishness of imagining that we are father and son. I look at his blue eyes and I think how they're the same, the exact same, as they were the day they first met mine on the stairway, except for that feverish light is gone from them. He's calm now, in the knowing of himself, making his reparations. And though barely a word has ever come between us that wasn't read by him from the pages of a book or a newspaper, we know one another the same as if we had a lifetime gave in one another's company. And I sit still, and I watch his eyes as they cross the pages, and I love him.

Acknowledgements

Thanks:

To Brian Langan; to Mary Ryan; to Joseph O'Connor and the Department of Creative Writing at the University of Limerick; to Sarah Bannan and the Arts Council of Ireland; to the people who read my books, for allowing me to be a writer; to everybody at my publishers and across the book trade who has worked to make my books successful; and to Anne Marie, Thomas and Lucy, the chambers of my heart.

A number of these stories previously appeared in other publications. 'Tommy and Moon' was commissioned and broadcast by BBC Radio 4; 'Losers Weepers' and 'Hanora Ryan, 1998' were published in *The Irish Times*; a shorter version of 'Grace' was published in The National Gallery of Ireland's book *Lines of Vision: Irish Writers on Art* (Thames and Hudson, 2014); and 'Meryl' was commissioned and published in the *Ogham Stone* Literary Journal, University of Limerick.